Journey to the King of Kings

Book 1: Exile

by Dennis Redline

Journey to the King of Kings
Book 1: Exile
by Dennis Redline

Printed in the United States of America

ISBN 9781615794423

Edited by Sharilyn Grayson
Illustration by Emily Metta Star

www.xulonpress.com

1/22/12

Deb,

I hope you enjoy the book!

Chapter 1

The Day Before

Grass, thick, luxurious green grass: Arden was lying in it on a hilltop just after sunset as the stars were starting to come out. At the moment he was not interested in a history or geography lesson. Perhaps neither are you, but if you don't know, then nothing about this story will make sense. Arden's home was the island kingdom of Caladen, a very large island isolated for the most part from the rest of the world. It lay just south of the Northern Sea, and to its east was the Great Sea, which no one had ever crossed. Due west of Caladen was the Shallow Sea with rocks and reefs that prevented any ship from sailing through it. West of the Shallow Sea stretched the "strange lands", as they are called. Somewhere beyond the "strange lands" was the land of Jeshuryn, wherein lay the City of Light, which was the home of the King of Kings. People from the strange lands came to Caladen to trade, but they could only sail into one port on the southern tip of the island. In the center of the country was a great city called Harran. At the center of this city was the even greater Cathedral of Light. Arden's family lived outside the city at the beginning of the farm lands, a good location for Arden's father Jacob, who was a farmer. A tall, strong man whose tough appearance might scare you at first, Jacob, like most other Caladenians, was a friendly and kind man. Caladen was mostly filled with fields, small towns, forests and streams. It was a pleasant land filled with kind people.

Anyway, Arden did not care about the geography of his home at present. Why? He was more interested in the girl, Sarah, who was lying next to him in the grass. Arden had lived on his father's farm all his life, but Sarah's family had moved to a house down the lane six months ago. He was completely smitten with her, and she felt pretty much the same way about him. They had walked up the hill hand in hand to see the sunset, and now they were lying in the grass. This excursion was the perfect way to end one of the last days of summer, when the day was hot, but the nights were starting to get cooler. Today was the kind of day where you know in your heart that the summer is about to end and soon the leaves will start to change color. At least the coolness of the evening was a good excuse to lie next to each other so closely.

Arden was seventeen, and this summer was his last after mid school. Soon he would start as an apprentice in his chosen field, botany and pharmacology. Ever since he was little, he had shown a knack with plants, all kinds of them, from garden vegetables to the herbs in the forest. People called him "garden Arden" sometimes as a good-natured nickname. He loved to explore the forests for different kind of plants. He had an amazing memory for their names and usages. One of his first teachers was his mother Heather, who also had this talent and had the great responsibility of tending the plants inside the Cathedral of Light. Arden was happy that he would soon start learning from one of the king's lore masters, a kind older man named Mr. Estely. Although Arden's studies would be challenging, he would be able to live at home most of the time, a situation which would mean living close to Sarah, who was a year younger and had one more year of mid school left.

The couple lay on the fresh smelling grass and looked up at the heavens. To the west shone a constellation of seven stars which some called "the hand of God" and others called "the stars of the king". One thousand years ago, unknown to the people of Caladen, a great war raged in the strange lands. At the end of that war, a ship wrecked on the southwest coast of Caladen, and the people nearby found a man on the shore. His clothes were torn, and he was barely alive, remaining unconscious for three days. Around his neck, he wore a pendant on a silver chain made from a strange metal that was not silver. The pendant had seven gems in the color and likeness of the seven stars. The survivor, whose name was Tendar, became the first real king of Caladen. For this reason, many years later, the stars became known as the "stars of the king" because of the pendant Tendar wore.

Arden could smell the sweet fragrance of the evening flowers on a gentle breeze, and for a moment his mind drifted back to the spring, when Sarah's family had moved into their house. At that time, he had heard that people were moving into the neighborhood, and he knew that his mother had planned a welcoming party for them at his house. Unfortunately, he had been invited to accompany Mr. Estely on a journey into the forest to look for several plants that only blossomed in the spring. That trip would take most of the day to complete, and the opportunity was so exciting that he really didn't care about missing the party. Arden and the lore master left at dawn and rode several hours north to the forest on a wagon pulled by two horses. Mr. Estely had many fascinating stories, and the ride passed much quicker than Arden thought possible. Mr. Estely also asked Arden many questions to get to know him better. The two left the wagon and horses at a village and ate a quick mid-morning breakfast before walking on a path to the forest. Out in the forest that day, they stumbled across a patch of stunning white flowers called angel's kiss. They had no medicinal value, but their beauty was not lost on either of the botanists. Mr. Estely found a small fruit on one of the plants which contained seeds. He was pleased about that discovery, because he could now grow angel's kiss in the cathedral's garden, where none grew at present. He let Arden carefully cut one of the flowers to bring back with him. Arden had intended to give it to his mother, who would really appreciate it. That day was perhaps one of the best days that Arden had spent in some time. He felt at home with Mr. Estely, and he had seen new plants and learned much about them while having fun. Master and student carefully stored on the wagon all the plants they had gathered and headed back.

The night was getting dark when the wagon finally got close to Arden's house. Arden dismounted, took his gear, and bid Mr. Estely farewell. As he walked down the lane from the main road, he grew more and more tired with each step. Then he stopped because he saw lights and heard music coming from up ahead. He was taken aback for a minute until he remembered the party. Then his irritation flared for a moment when he realized that he would not have a quiet house in which he could rest. The irritation woke him up a bit, and as he came closer, he could smell food and hear people talking. The party was actually winding down, and people were coming out of the house and starting down the lane to their homes. They greeted him, and he replied in turn. His mother met him at the door and called him inside to inquire about his day. Her eyes seemed to carry some hidden excitement, which distracted him for a moment. He carefully unloaded his pack and took out some of the plants that would need water and planting immediately. He started to feel tired again. As he was taking out the angel's kiss to surprise his mother, he heard his father approach. Two strangers accompanied his father, a man and a woman, obviously the new neighbors.

"This is my son Arden," his father said, introducing him to the two adults. Arden stood politely and shook their hands.

"Sarah, it's time to go," called the woman to the other room. *Who is Sarah?* he wondered. Then, before he could ponder further, a girl came around the corner.

Now, many people don't necessarily believe in love at first sight. Neither did Arden, or Sarah, for that matter. He was immediately taken by her blue eyes. Looking into them was like discovering a beautiful flower. She was (to him) the most beautiful girl he had ever seen. Then suddenly he felt awkward, standing there in front of both his and her parents, not knowing what to say. Thank goodness that Sarah came over to him, shook his hand, and said hello.

"Arden's been out on a trip to the forest today," his mother said, a comment which made Arden feel more stupid, because the guests were bound to have known his whereabouts from an earlier conversation.

Then, it happened. He felt like he was a puppet the way his hand just lifted, not out of conscious thought, but of reaction. Luckily, before he could even second guess his own actions, he gave Sarah the flower. "This is for you," he said, or something close.

"It's beautiful," she said, holding it up for everyone to see. Then suddenly, it seemed, the guests of honor were out the door and on their way home. Arden's mother tended to the other plants that Arden brought home. Arden went to bed and fell fast asleep. He could not remember his dreams that night, except one part. He was in an orchard, with blossoms falling all around him like snow. Sarah came forward, took his hand, and led him down the path past the trees into a garden of flowers.

Tonight as they walked back down from the hill, Arden felt like this day was the best day of his entire life. The morning had started with the anticipation of people arriving for the large celebration at Arden's house that Arden's family held every summer's end. Family and neighbors would come over to enjoy an abundance of food, play many games, sing, and tell family stories: things that had happened during the past year and hopes for the future. Every year, after a large evening meal, the men lit a bonfire. When the fire died down, the younger children were put to bed. The adults would talk and sometimes sing again. The younger adults might have their own conversations or go inside for other games. The evening would end for the adults and anyone else still awake with a time of prayer.

Arden and Sarah snuck away after the evening meal to see the sunset by themselves. They thought that nobody would notice because of the number of people gathered, but both Arden's mother and Sarah's saw them from the kitchen window. They looked at each other and smiled.

"I remember when she was just taking her first steps," Sarah's mother said, laughing. "I guess we're getting old."

"Soon you'll both be grandmothers, "said Arden's father, who had walked in with Sarah's father behind him.

"Whatever you say, grandpa," said Arden's mother.

They all laughed together.

Chapter 2

The Cathedral at Harran

The next day was also fun, because many people who had come stayed for the night. A large gathering remained for the noon meal. Another beautiful day blessed the celebration with a dark blue sky and white, puffy clouds. Flowers bloomed by the house, and ripe vegetables still filled the garden. Although yesterday Arden had been oblivious to the chatter, now he did notice some relatives pointing out him and Sarah and speaking of impending marriage. At one point when Sarah was with him, she turned to him and smiled when someone mentioned their wedding. Arden actually blushed, but when he made eye contact with Sarah, a moment of seriousness held Arden. He knew the day would come when he would ask her to marry him. Sarah knew so as well. Most of the overnight guests left in the afternoon, and Arden did quite a bit of cleanup work to help. Sarah helped as well, along with her younger brother and sister. Arden's mother reminded him not to stay up too late because the two of them were going to the city the next day to work at the cathedral. The remaining guests, Arden's family, and Sarah's family shared the evening meal outside and talked until the sun was setting. Everyone cleaned the supper dishes, and Sarah's family left. Arden's parents stayed outside talking with their other guests, and Arden went to his room to prepare for the next day. He decided to bring a small book on plant care with him in case he needed it.

Despite the long day, Arden did not sleep well that night. His mind was racing, mostly about Sarah, but also because he was going to the city and to the Cathedral. He took awhile to get to sleep, but at last he slept and dreamed fitfully. His dreams went something like this: *Sarah-sky-Sarah-sunset-stars-plants-kiss-Sarah-Cathedral-grass-holding hands-happy-walking on the lane-Sarah-noise-Sarah-fields-more noise-light-morning already?* Yes, morning had come, and his mother had to wake him twice to get him up. He barely had time for a quick breakfast before they were off.

The walk to the city gates was three miles, and the Cathedral was another two miles. Although the day was early, the sun already felt hot; today was another day where summer would fight to hold on. Arden felt sweat on his forehead from the sun at mile two. Today was not the first time that he and his mother had gone to the city to work. Sometimes they would talk on the way, and other days they would not say much. Today was a quiet day. The one thing Arden did confirm with his mother was that they could stop at Sarah's family store after their work was finished. His mother had much on her mind as well, because the king would be at the Cathedral today to meet with all of the senior workers. Most outside people would not understand that Caladen's king was not just the king, but also the spiritual leader of his people who led them in worship at the Cathedral. Many other churches had their own pastors, but the king was the leader of them all: King Arcturus the Wise, as he was called. But he (and everyone) bowed to the King of Kings. His mother was not afraid of the meeting; she was looking forward to it. The king always had some wisdom and insight to share with the workers. Although he was king, he always made you feel important in whatever job you had: not just important, but worthy. The kings of Caladen were filled with the spirit of God, and they lovingly and justly ruled with authority. They tried their best to follow the example of the King of Kings, also known as the Son of the Lord Most High.

Arden did not completely understand how the king became the king or everything about the Scriptures and the teachings. He knew that this year, from the time he was seventeen to his eighteenth birthday, he would learn a lot more. When a citizen turned eighteen, he needed to perform a ceremony called the "Day of Choosing" within one year. Usually the ceremony occurred en masse to save time and create a bigger celebration. The law required each person to swear allegiance to the Lord Most High, the King of Kings (His Son), and the Spirit of God. Every celebrant recited certain Scriptures and gave an oath to the king of the land to serve his country and fellow citizens. The ceremony was a joyous time. Mostly, that is. Anyone who would not give his allegiance would be banished from the land to the strange lands across the sea. But people rarely left the kingdom for this or any other reason. Occasionally, mostly near or in the port, someone would decide to leave. Once he made that choice, he could not come back. It was the law.

When Arden was little, six teenagers, three boys and three girls, caused the largest scandal in hundreds of years when they refused to take the oath and were banished. Arden could barely remember neighbors coming over at night, people praying and weeping over this decision. Arden was bewildered then at how these six teens that his parents didn't even know could upset them so. Sometimes Arden wondered why anyone would make the choice to leave the country, and he wondered what happened to the banished teens. Did they regret their decision? Some children in school said that they were dead. He asked his mother once, but she would not even speculate on what happened to them. All she would say was, "Why don't you pray for them?"

Arden and his mother finally reached the Cathedral, after stopping several times along the way. Every time that Arden saw the Cathedral, he was filled with awe. This structure wasn't an impersonal Cathedral made from cold stone. It was vibrant and full of life. The building was white with a grand entrance where stairs led up to two huge doors of wood inlaid with gold. The massive main worship area could seat thousands easily in a half circle of tiered seating. On both sides of the sanctuary was also a tiered area where musicians were staged, and on the center platform was an altar with elaborate designs. Behind the altar on the next highest tier was the throne of the king, flanked by eight other thrones: one for the Queen and seven for the elders of the church. Above this level was the throne for the King of Kings. Three sets of stairs led up to this throne and two great white trees rose on each side. The Cathedral was full of plants and trees. Near the ceiling of the great hall, strategically placed windows let in light.

Arden would usually inspect the trees in the courtyard and the gardens, depending on the season, while his mother would check the plants inside the worship area. Then she would check the outer rooms. Usually, mother and son would meet somewhere in the rooms. Then they would climb the tower to check the water supplies. A series of catch basins collected rain water from the roof, and several hidden channels carried this water down into an outer room. Workers in the Cathedral would use this water for the plants. The fill controls were up in the tower. Some people would not like having to climb all of the stairs, but the view from the top was breathtaking. Today, as things would have it, students of Mr. Estely had already inspected the outside trees and gardens as part of an exam. So Arden got to go right into the worship area and start there, while his mother went to meet with the workers and the king. Although checking on plants might not seem like it would take a long time, the building was full of plants. The worship area was bright and alive with color.

Arden decided to start with the altar. He would never have been allowed to walk there if not for this reason. Normally a guard watched the worship area, but not always. Today the guards were with the king. What really caught Arden's attention was the throne of the King of Kings. He had never seen it up close, and he immediately walked straight up to that tier. The throne looked large and menacing from a distance, but up close he realized that it was also very beautiful. The outside was polished stone with intricate carvings that were not clearly visible from a distance. At the top of the throne, two wings of white stretched outward from an image of a crown in the center. The carving was so different looking that Arden could not easily describe it. Yet it was so fascinating that he could hardly keep from staring at it. The whole throne was a symbol of the majesty of God. Then words popped into his head as he remembered a teacher speaking them, a very important law: NO ONE SHALL SIT UPON THIS THRONE BUT THE KING OF KINGS. A sudden weariness came over him as he stood there watching it. He felt a desire to sit on the throne. *Why must only the King of Kings sit there?* he thought. The throne looked so inviting that he had to turn away from it, looking out into the worship area. He felt almost a sense of vertigo as he viewed everything from this vantage point. Even the altar below felt like it was so far down that he would surely die if he fell over the edge. He instinctively backed up until he hit something solid behind him. He could never quite explain what happened next. He pushed backwards, and his arms reached behind him and picked him up onto the throne. For an instant, he realized what he had done and panicked. At the same time, a sense of peace flooded over him, overwhelming him. Instantly he fell asleep.

He remained there unconscious for quite some time until a cleaning woman entered from a side door. A scream rang out in the sanctuary when she finally saw him. Guards came running. The senior workers, the kings' envoy, and the king came rushing in to find a teen sitting on the throne of the King of Kings. Silence filled the room, and then outrage. "Wake him up!" someone shouted. "Get him out of there!" another voice demanded. Arden woke to the noise and found himself sitting there with fifty people staring at him.

"Arrest him!" the chief guard cried. Arden sprang to his feet as two guards came from either side and grabbed him by the arms. "Get the Constable!" said the chief guard. All eyes turned to the king for direction. "With your permission, my Lord," said the chief guard, bowing to the king.

"Yes, let the Constable take him" said the king. "We will convene the council immediately to determine what action must be taken."

Chapter 3

Jail and Sentence

The jail at Harran was in its own way a testament to the changes in the country over the last nine hundred years. As the city grew in size, many of the older buildings at its center changed in function and form. The jail was built from a building that was originally a large stable for horses; when the city converted the building, each stall became a jail cell. The adjacent building that had been the army headquarters became the police headquarters. Builders replaced the wood in each of the ten jail cells with stone. As time went on, the need for ten jail cells simply did not exist, and the building was further subdivided into a police building and fire brigade. As the new religion spread through the land, the need for police at all dwindled. The police force was mostly used for emergencies to help the people. The constable lived at the headquarters during the week, and another policeman took over on the weekends. Eventually, the constable and his family moved upstairs above the jail. So the downstairs consisted of an office and three cells. Well, as three jail cells weren't needed, the city turned one into an area for the officers to eat and the other into a bedroom. During bad storms in the winter, most of the staff would stay in town rather than venture home. The wife of one constable realized one day that these former cells were cold and damp and needed some remodeling. So the police laid wood floors and walls over the stone and made the cells much more hospitable.

During a severe winter the same year, the headquarters became a temporary shelter when two houses burned down. The building was then full, including the one remaining jail cell. The constable's wife then realized that the remaining cell would have to be changed as well, although making a jail cell pleasant seemed sort of a foolish idea. However, the cell was an eyesore, and keeping the stranded people there was an embarrassment. So in the late spring, the police decided to overhaul it. Again, they installed wood over the floors and walls and built a smaller room in the cell to shield the open toilet. A new bed and a small desk and chair furnished the room. When it was all said and done, everyone who saw the cell remarked on how good it looked. The cell would now serve as another bedroom when needed. But one problem was not discovered for some time. In the late summer, the police decided to repaint some of the building trim with black paint. With the leftover paint, they decided to paint the bars in front of the cell also. Then they realized that the cell door would not close. The wood floor in front of the doorway was slightly warped, and so the door would swing to close and then get stuck. As this flaw was rather embarrassing, the police decided to keep it quiet with the hope that maybe the warping was seasonal and that in the winter the door would close. However, in the winter the door would not close either.

So the whole story became a police secret that only a few knew. It turned into a ritual secret that was passed from one generation of constables to another. The police did have two options available, though. They made a chain with a lock that would hold the door closed. Also, they installed eyelets in the walls so that a prisoner could be chained and not escape.

When Arden arrived at the jail, the constable was faced with these two choices: chain Arden to the wall or trust that he would not try to escape. The constable did not trust the chain to hold the door close enough so that Arden could not squeeze his way out. He did not want to chain the boy, though; the treatment seemed too harsh. He escorted Arden to the cell, and Arden immediately fell on the bed facing the wall. The constable made the decision to secure the chain on the door. This boy was obviously not a hardened criminal bent on escape.

Arden remained motionless most of the afternoon in a state of shock and despair. He was filled with emotion so intense that after a while it physically exhausted him, and he fell asleep. By now, word of his offense had spread through the city and reached Arden's father as well. A flurry of activity surrounded the cathedral, and finally the captain deployed the king's guards to keep the crowd from loitering in the courtyard and to answer any questions. The high council was summoned as well as Arden's family. His father and mother arrived and were admitted along with Mr. Estely, who wanted to speak on Arden's behalf. Sarah and her mother waited outside in the courtyard, and they were also called inside. The crowd that surrounded the cathedral was not hostile but curious and concerned. After the initial shock wore off and the truth of what happened was revealed, the crowds split into smaller groups and began to pray. Many left to go back to their families and neighborhoods to relay the news and gather in prayer. Many of the older people had flashbacks of the incident with the six teens that had occurred years ago. Some fasted. Arden still slept.

Finally, Arden woke with a start. Tears flowed down his face as he sat on the edge of the bed with his head in his hands. He could smell the aroma of food coming from upstairs, and it really smelled good. The constable's wife was quite a cook. Although Arden did not feel hungry, his stomach suddenly growled in hunger. He sat in silence for quite some time, not knowing what to do. He could hear the floor creaking upstairs as people moved about. Finally, he heard the sound of chairs on the floor and then dishes clinking as the constable's family began their evening meal. The sun was setting, and the sky was getting dark outside. For a moment, all was silent again, and then Arden heard a chair. Someone got up from the table and was coming downstairs. Actually, two people were coming. The constable and his wife appeared at the cell bars. Arden was too ashamed even to look at them. The constable unlocked the chain holding the door and opened it. The constable's wife brought in a plate of food and set it on the small table in the cell along with a cup of water. Arden looked up at them and saw compassion in their faces, not the condemnation that he expected. Now tears really began to flow from his eyes.

The constable and his wife sat on each side of him. "You have to eat something," said the wife, putting her arms around him.

"Son," said the constable, "we all make mistakes, some worse than others. I could tell that you are not a dishonest person from the moment I set eyes upon you. I know that things may seem hopeless now, but tomorrow is another day. Of all the places that you could have committed a crime, our land is the fairest, and the Lord Most High is merciful."

The couple consoled him briefly, and then they ended up taking Arden upstairs and let him eat supper with them at the table. The constable had strict orders not to allow Arden visitors, and as he had not heard otherwise at this point, he assumed that nobody would be allowed to see Arden. After supper, the family sat with Arden by the fireplace upstairs. The constable and his wife told him several stories to lighten the mood and then they asked Arden many questions about himself. At first, answering was hard, but soon he told them much of his life and adventures. When he got to the part about Sarah moving in, he suddenly came back to the reality of his situation. He just could not bring himself to talk about her for fear of crying. Sensing that something was troubling him, they did not ask any more but changed the subject. By now, the night was getting late, and soon everyone would need to get to bed. Once again, the couple assured Arden that, although things were not well, what was done was done and that he would need to face the council in the morning. However, the council and the king were fair and honorable. The couple said goodnight to Arden, and the constable returned him to the cell, securing the door with the chain.

Arden fell into a restless sleep but soon woke up with a start. Once again he felt guilt and sadness overwhelm him, and he just lay awake for some time with his heart pounding and his mind racing with unanswered questions. At the same time he was experiencing this distress, the members of the high council were in session in deep discussions concerning him. His mother and father were sitting in their house with their friends and neighbors around to give support. They were about to enter into prayer. Sarah was standing outside on the hilltop nearby in the cool breeze, the very same hilltop where she and Arden had just gone to watch the sunset. Tears streamed down her face, and she became dizzy as everything turned blurry. Her mind was also racing with questions and confusion over the day's events. Her mother did not go after her as she ran out the door. She knew that her child needed to be alone for a while. Almost out of nowhere, Sarah saw a man approach her. For a moment, she thought he was her father or Arden's. When the man reached her, she could not recognize him at first. Then she realized that he was the king. She immediately fell to her knees. He took her by the hand and lifted her back to her feet. She fell forward and embraced him, not caring if he was the king or not. For a long while, they just stood still. Eventually, Sarah stopped crying, and a sense of peace came over her. The king said nothing and did not move until he somehow knew that she was ready to go. He put his arm over her shoulder as they walked down the lane to Arden's house, where everyone had gathered. He walked her to the door.

Before leaving, he turned to her and said, "Sarah, may the peace of the Lord Most High be with you." He turned and left her standing outside the door. Sarah's mother heard a voice outside and came to the door in a few minutes. When she saw Sarah standing there, she went out to her. Sarah hugged her mother, and then the two went inside. Her mother did not see the king.

"We are about to pray," said her mother. "Why don't you take a moment to get ready?"

Arden's mother brought Sarah upstairs to the bathroom. Sarah looked in the mirror. Her eyes were bloodshot from crying, and her hair was messy. She ran her hand over her hair and noticed that the top was wet. She took a brush and brushed it and then tied it up in back. She washed her face and drank a glass of water. Taking a deep breath, she found herself calmer now. Seeing the king had been like a dream, and she did not want to mention it now. She went downstairs and joined the prayer circle. Later, when the prayer was over, her mother took her home. Her father stayed with the other adults, who would probably be up very late. Only after Sarah was in bed and just about to fall asleep did she realize why her hair was wet on top. The king had been crying, too.

The next morning, the council hall was filled with people when Arden was brought in. In the front on a raised platform were the chairs for the high council, with the king's throne in the center. In front of this platform was a smaller and lower one with two small tables with chairs. One of them had a gavel with a stand for it. Before this platform was a table with three chairs, facing the council. Behind this table were the seats for everyone else. Arden entered from the back, with the constable and another officer walking on each side of him. He was thankful that they did not put restraints on him. The constable thought that the precaution was completely unnecessary, and being a kind man at heart, he did not want to embarrass the boy any more than needed. The three walked through the center aisle, stood in front of the three chairs, and remained standing, as the constable had instructed them. Guards stood solidly at the back entrance and at each of the side entrances in the front of the room. The room was full of people, and Arden did not think that anyone else could fit inside. People were even standing in the back because there were not enough chairs. Arden did not look to the side as he walked in, despite the urge to see a familiar face. When he reached the front, he did not want to turn and face the crowd.

"All rise for the king!" shouted one of the guards. The people stood in complete silence as the king and the high council entered. Two royal guards of high position sat at the tables before the council, ready to carry out any commands. The councilman with the gavel banged it on the table and called the court to order. The crowd was seated but Arden and his escorts remained standing.

The king stood up. He surveyed the crowd and then looked at the three before him. Then he spoke. "This hearing is not a trial in the conventional sense, as the guilt has already been established through many witnesses. We stand here today to issue our decision on the penalty of this offense. However, before we pass sentence, does the accused have anything to say on his behalf?"

Arden felt all eyes turn towards him. He wanted to say so many things, but he felt like a voice inside was telling him to remain silent. He shook his head no.

"Very well," said the king. "You may be seated." Arden and the officers took their seats. When they were seated, the king began, "Before we pass sentence today, certain information needs to be made public to all of the people present here today. The council has been in discussion and prayer for the entire night. In the history of Caladen, someone unauthorized has sat on the throne of the King of Kings in only two other instances. Indeed, the first was nine hundred years ago, when the evil Mordeck sat on the throne and declared himself above the God we serve. His rebellion was crushed, and he was killed outside these very walls. This command from the Lord not to sit on the throne became a civil law from that moment forward, but no penalty was ever specified. Death was assumed to be the only option." At that point, Sarah could hold back no longer, and she burst into tears and began sobbing out loud. People in the front started whispering, and those in the back were straining to see what was going on up front.

"Order!" cried the guard, banging the gavel on the table.

"Calm yourself, child," said one of the council, not in a mean way, but in a compassionate tone.

To everyone's amazement, the king came down to where Sarah was seated. By now she was sitting with her head down in her hands.

"Sarah, trust in the Lord Most High," said the king in a soft voice that only a few could hear, and he lifted up her head. Tears still rolled down her face, but the sobbing stopped. Arden's mother had tears on her face as well. Arden felt his throat tighten with sadness and guilt, but he did not cry. The king's action quieted the crowd and brought them back to order. He returned to his position on the platform.

He continued. "The second instance was fifty years ago, when a young child sat on the throne. Because the child was only five, the responsibility fell on the parents of that child. The judgment of the council at that time was to exile the parents from the city with no possibility of return. That punishment was just. However, we are faced with a dilemma. We do not believe that Arden's intent was evil, yet we cannot claim for him the simple ignorance of a child." Looking directly at Arden, the king said, "Quite frankly, we do not know why you have broken the law. You are too close to the age of decision for us to hold your parents responsible, even though they would gladly take your place. A long time has passed since the council has had to spend so much time in discussion and prayer to reach agreement. Please rise." Arden and the two officers stood.

"Arden, the decision of the council is that you are to be sent from this land to the land of Jeshuryn to ask the forgiveness of the King of Kings personally and to face his judgment. When you have completed this task, if his judgment allows, you may return to our land." Gasps came from several in the crowd, and a low murmur came from the back as people talked to each other in low voices, most just confirming what they had heard. Once again, the court was called to order.

The king continued. "The trading season is almost at an end, and not many ships are left that will leave our shores now. As is well known, we do not trust outsiders either, especially with business concerning the King of Kings. However, one ship currently here has a trustworthy captain and some merchants that are our distant brothers from Jeshuryn. Even now, messengers are riding to the port to seek your passage on this ship." Turning to Arden, he said, "We believe that this ship will take you across the sea and start you on your quest. You will leave today for the port, escorted by the constable. This court is adjourned."

"All rise!" shouted the guard. The people stood in silence as the officers took Arden out the side door and back to the jail. The trial happened so quickly that he did not get a chance to look at Sarah or his mother's face.

Chapter 4

Old Harbor

Back at the jail, Arden sat with the constable in the room outside the cell. The constable's wife was upstairs packing whatever items she thought the constable would need for the journey to the port. The constable told Arden that he would escort him to the town of Old Harbor by the sea. Arden took some comfort in the promise of somewhat familiar companionship, but he was still in a state of shock at the thought that he would have to leave so quickly. Although the king's guards were posted outside, no crowd had gathered. Arden hoped his parents and Sarah would come. He heard the police horses trotting up outside and knew that he would leave soon. The constable went outside and conferred with the guard while his wife sat next to Arden with her arm around his shoulder. The constable came back in. Behind him were Arden's parents and Sarah. Arden stood up, and his mother threw her arms around him tightly. His father joined in the embrace. Like the constable, Jacob and Heather knew that the sentence could have been far worse and that, realistically, Arden could be home in a year. They told Sarah so, but she could not comprehend the seemingly interminable time. The constable went outside and came back in a few minutes later. "It's time," he said, and he went outside again with his wife and the bag that she had packed for the trip. Arden's mother kissed him, and both parents reassured him that they still loved him and always would. They told him to hurry back as soon as possible. Then they stepped outside, leaving only Sarah. Arden didn't know what to say. He started to stammer a few words, but Sarah embraced him tightly. As he felt her hot tears on his face, tears came from his eyes as well. Her body was trembling, and he felt lost in the moment. The constable came in again, and although he felt badly, he had to interrupt. "Arden, it's time to go."

Although Arden hated to let go, he relaxed his embrace, and Sarah did the same. They parted and stood face to face. Although Arden could sense the constable's impatience, he dared one last kiss. It was short but sweet. He took her by the hand, and they went outside.

"I'll wait for you," she whispered in his ear before they went through the door.

"I will return as soon as I can," he said to Sarah and his parents.

The constable led Arden into the waiting carriage. Sarah's parents were also there, and her mother had her arm around Sarah as they watched. Arden looked out the small back window as the constable gave the word to proceed. Arden saw his parents and Sarah's parents, but his gaze was primarily on Sarah. The look of sadness and loss had returned to her, and tears rolled down her face. Then the carriage lurched forward, and soon he could not see them anymore. The constable said nothing, and he and Arden rode in silence.

The clouds rolled in and dampened the hot sun as Arden and the constable rode south on the road to Old Harbor. The rest of the group consisted of four guards on horses, two in front and two behind the carriage that contained the constable and Arden. To have the guards was unnecessary, but the law was the law. Arden was relieved when the group finally left the city and the crowds of people lining the road. Some had been standing and staring with an air of disbelief about them. Others were praying. Some were kneeling, others speaking loudly. A breeze blew, and its coolness was refreshing. Arden had never been on this road, although he knew its significance to the people of Caladen. The constable, who loved history and telling a good story, refreshed Arden's memory as they traveled the road.

A thousand years ago, when Tendar finally woke from unconsciousness, he warned the people of the harbor that a fleet of ships would arrive soon with troops that would invade the land. Most of the people did not believe him and considered his warning the ramblings of a crazy man. But a few of the wisest among the people knew that he was telling the truth. However, they really did not know what to do, even if Tendar was telling the truth, except tell everyone to leave the town. They decided on two things. The first would be to send Tendar with an escort (that included most of them) north to the city of Harran, where the ruler of the region resided. The second was to issue a stern warning to the people to post lookouts and flee to the hills if a fleet arrived. But the people were not convinced that a fleet would arrive and attack them for no reason, and they were divided on this order. They tried to post lookouts, but the few they could muster were not one hundred percent focused on their duty. Three more days passed before a fleet of ships arrived, just as Tendar had foretold.

Meanwhile, Tendar and his escorts rode north with all the speed that they could muster at Tendar's bidding. Those around him began to recognize that he possessed the natural authority and skills of a leader. When the warning party reached Harran, the men made their way to see the leader of the region, a man named Jaden. To note the timing of their arrival is ironic. At that time, Caladen had split into two regions which were on the brink of war over some minor territorial disputes. They had much hostility towards each other over things long past. But the two leaders of the regions, Jaden and Jarius, both wise men of honor who realized that such a war would really cause more damage then it was worth for either region, were looking for a reason to cease hostilities without seeming weak to their people. They were both in the main hall when they heard an uproar from the outside chambers. Eventually, they admitted Tendar and spoke to him. Tendar spoke for several hours to them about who he was, why he was there, and what was to come. Very few were present to hear his words, but what he said convinced the leaders that their land was in danger. This threat also gave them a reason to postpone their own pending war and seek an alliance. The next day, Tendar rode south with Jaden and an army of ten thousand men, and Jaden sent word to enlist another force to leave as soon as possible. Jarius sent word north to send as many men as could be spared south to reinforce Harran and to march farther south into battle. He also rode with Jaden and Tendar. By now, four days had passed.

At the harbor, a fleet of sixty ships arrived with twenty thousand men. Many in the town fled when they saw the ships, and the ones who stayed behind were slaughtered without mercy. Only a day elapsed before all the troops were ashore and organized. Their captain wanted them to be on the move as quickly as possible, for the harbor town was surrounded on all sides by steep hills, like a three-sided bowl. But he did not want to leave until all the provisions were unloaded and their beachhead was firmly established. He sent scouts out to survey the land and to gather any information that they could. He was not aware either that their landing had been foretold or that an army was coming his way. By now, the ten thousand men of Caladen were mobilized, while another eight thousand from the city were less than a day behind and fifteen thousand more from the north were rallied and leaving.

In the present, the clouds got darker, and a light rain began to fall on the police convoy, which stopped for the evening in a small town. Arden concluded that the rain kept any audience away, or perhaps these people here had not heard the news. In reality, the riders that went before them had informed the town leaders. But most of the townspeople were at home with their families for the evening meal. The town did not have a jail cell; so the police party stayed in the village inn. The constable and Arden ate in the constable's room. The guards were the king's men, and they did not interact too much with Arden or the constable. The guards agreed that if the door to Arden's room was locked, there would not be any reason to post a guard outside. The constable agreed, and he took the key from the lock on the inside of the room and locked Arden in from the outside.

The second day of the journey to Old Harbor was a cloudy day with a steady breeze. The roads were still damp and wet in places from the storm the night before. The group rode past fields and stone walls. The constable told Arden many things about the areas through which they were riding as well as stories from his youth. The talk passed the time and made the journey better for Arden. The group stopped for lunch at midday and later at another inn for the night.

Just after Arden had been locked in his room and was preparing for bed, he heard the sound of a lone horse arriving. Although he could not see the rider from his window, he heard him enter the hotel, and a flurry of activity followed. Arden could not help but wonder if this fuss was related to him. Maybe the ship had left already, and they would have to go back. He heard people coming upstairs and knocking at the constable's door. The constable answered in a loud voice, annoyed at being disturbed, probably for some trivial reason. But then he was quiet, and Arden could only hear low voices which were so low that Arden could not understand them. Arden heard footsteps outside his door and realized that he was standing in the middle of the room with anxiety growing. He heard the key in the lock, and his door was unlocked and opened. In front of the door was a tall figure with a black cloak around him. Arden saw the crown and was shocked that the king was at his door.

"May I come in?" he asked.

Arden just nodded his head yes in shocked silence. The king entered and sat in one of the two chairs by a small table in the room. The door closed behind him, and Arden realized that guards stood watch outside. The king motioned for Arden to sit in the other chair. Arden complied without thinking.

"You have no need to be alarmed, Arden," said the king. "I wanted to speak to you, and a meeting is much more inconspicuous this way. I have much that I would like to say, but the need to be concise is also important. First of all, how are you?"

"Um, okay, I guess," said Arden uncertainly.

The king chuckled. "Well, given the circumstances, I guess I could not expect any other answer. I can see that this chain of events is shocking for you, and I am truly sorry that your path has to lie this way. Were any other way possible, we would have chosen it. But take heart; far worse results could have come from this offense. You may not see so now, but I hope that someday you will.

"As I said in the trial, as it were, years ago a young child sat in the throne as well. What you and many others do not know is that I was that child." Arden's eyes widened in surprise. The king continued, "I don't really remember doing it, and I could not tell you why I did it. I suppose that what happened is the same with you, and I will not ask you why you repeated my offense. But you have to understand that consequences will flow from your actions. My parents were kind and loving, but being banished from their beloved city and home caused them tremendous hurt. My action brought shame upon them, and they took a long time to get over that humiliation. I was sent to live with my grandparents for many years. They were very strict, and I hated living with them, even more because I did not understand what had happened or why I was there. Recovering from my separation from my family also took many years for me as well. In retrospect, my grandparents raised me well, and eventually I went back to live with my mother. My father was killed in an accident, and I never saw him again after the day of my judgment. Many things have happened since then, both bad and good, and I cannot tell you everything. My mother could not come to the city when I was crowned king and could never attend any of the services in the cathedral. So you see, consequences followed for what I did, but not just for myself." Arden remained silent, but he realized that the king was right. Although he was hurting, his parents and Sarah were also hurting just as badly.

The king paused for a moment and then continued. "The reason that I am here is that our nation is at a critical time in its history. The council and I, as well as many other people that fellowship with the Spirit of the Lord Most High, feel that something is going to happen soon. Something good! This expectation makes sending you away even more painful for us. We also wrestled with the fact that none of us, including myself, have ever traveled outside this land. We are sure, though, that we are putting you in the right hands and that the men to whom we are entrusting you are honorable men. Captain Stephens and his crew will deliver you safely to the strange lands. A merchant named Hershel, who is traveling with his sons, will take you to Jeshuryn. However, be warned; be careful who you trust. An evil queen in the strange lands despises the Lord Most High; she will not appreciate anyone from our country passing through her lands. Do not be afraid, but be prudent in your dealings with others. I do not know what road you will take, but I will tell you that anyone that

Hershel and his sons trust, you can trust. I know I am telling you a lot right now, but I must also tell you more."

"When Tendar came ashore a thousand years ago, he wore a pendant around his neck with the seven stars. Since that time, each successive king has been entrusted with its care. Before he died, Tendar prophesied that three people would sit upon the great throne: an evil man who made a choice, a child who was careless, and a young man who would be banished from the land. The latter must be given the pendant to wear on his journey." The king stood, took a box from his cloak, and opened it, revealing the pendant inside. He took it out and held it up in front of Arden. Even in the dim light of the room, the pendant shone brightly. The seven stars sparkled. Three of them were white, three were yellowish, one was clear, and one was blue. The clear one and the blue one were in the center, and pattern and colors matched the stars in the sky exactly. Arden did not know what to say or do. Then the king put the pendant over Arden's head, and it rested around his neck.

"Tuck it inside your shirt," said the king. "The direction given has been passed along all of these years, and you must obey it at all times. You must not let anyone know that you are wearing it: not a single person. Not the constable, the guards, the captain of the ship, the merchants, or anyone else that you encounter. When the time is right, it will be revealed to the ones that need to see it. So, to whom will you show it?"

"Nobody," said Arden.

"Good," said the king. "Finally, I have just one more thing to say, and I don't know how to say it easily. Arden, do not let your quest be driven by the desire to return home to family and friends. Rather, continue learning the ways of the Lord Most High. Let His Spirit guide you on this journey. By saying what I am, I don't mean that I think that you will fail, but rather that you must remember why you are on this journey. Your goal is to reach the King of Kings, and you must prepare for that goal. I don't know what will happen when you arrive, but your fate rests in His hands. In reality, it does anyway."

Before the king left, he shared a small meal with Arden and then prayed with him and for him. He embraced Arden, and then he left as quietly as he had come. Arden heard him ride away into the night. Arden felt a peace around him after the king prayed, and he fell asleep right away.

The third day, Arden and his guard reached the outer limits of Old Harbor and stopped when they reached the gate of the town above the harbor. The constable dismounted the carriage and went into a small brick building on the right. He emerged ten minutes later and let Arden out of the carriage. Arden felt good to get his feet back on the ground after the ride. The sun was shining through the haze above in the late morning.

"Let's take a walk and stretch our legs," the constable said.

The group walked past the brick house but not into the town, as Arden had suspected. A path led them through an alley with stone walls on either side. At the end of the alley was a staircase on the right, leading up one flight to a landing, and then up another, longer flight of stairs to the top. They found themselves on top of a wall looking down into the harbor. Over the wall blew a strong breeze, cool and refreshing. As Arden looked down into the harbor, the first thing he noticed (which he couldn't help) was the series of walls that surrounded it. A sheer cliff rose at the front of the town, and a wall crowned the top of it. Flanking the wall on either side were two larger walls, like the rampart of a castle. Arden and the guards were on the wall at the right. From this vantage point, Arden saw clearly that the walls were there to keep the harbor isolated. Two roads, one on each side, led up to the cliff. What he couldn't see was a tunnel at the base of the cliff which led up to the town at the top of the wall. All traffic to and from the harbor would go by this road.

As Arden looked down past the town, he could see the top of one ship in the port. *That must be the ship I'm to sail on,* he thought. Then he looked past the town, out towards the sea. From here, the sea stretched out as far as he could see. He could hardly imagine crossing it to anywhere. The constable was also looking out in the harbor, imaging what seeing the black ships in the harbor and an army massing below those many years ago must have been like. Even more amazing must have been the Caladenian army led by the mighty Tendar, Jaden, and Jarius. The constable wanted to stop and tell Arden about the great victory and the great cost of the battle, but he had no time.

The group walked down the road from the town into the tunnel under the cliff. At each end of the tunnel were iron gates. From the top of the road, Arden could see large rocks piled above the first gate in a strange pattern, but he did not realize that these rocks could be triggered to come crashing down into the tunnel, to seal it in case of an invasion. The defense had never been triggered, and moss covered most of the lower rocks.

At the bottom gate, small buildings clustered on both sides, and guards and other official-looking men walked around. Some were inspecting the carts coming from the harbor. Others were checking the papers of people waiting to get through the gate. Arden and the guards approached the gate and waited in line behind two carts and three people carrying small sacks. When Arden's group reached the front, the constable handed the official their papers. The official glanced at the papers, looked up at the men briefly, and told them to wait for a minute. He went into the building and returned with another man who had a uniform similar to the constable's, as he was the constable of the town of Old Harbor.

"We'll take it from here," the officer said to the men escorting Arden. He stamped the papers to signify the prisoner transfer and handed them back to the constable.

"Give us a minute, please," said the constable from Harran. He turned to Arden and put his hands on Arden's shoulders. "God be with you, my son." He gave him a hug, and then he turned and started back up the hill. Arden felt his heart sink again, not as badly as before, but it hurt nonetheless.

The new constable said, "Come along son," and he and Arden started down the stone road towards the town. The new constable was a tall man with a stern face, but not a mean one. You could tell that he was a strong man by his build and that he was a leader of men by his bearing. When he saw Arden, he felt sympathy, a reaction which he had not expected. He was used to dealing with a rougher clientele: hardened sailors from across the sea and the occasional townsperson turned criminal. This prisoner, just a teen looking fragile and scared, was a new experience for him. He normally put these prisoners in irons and led them through the streets as sort of a last punishment at leaving this fair land. For any prisoners to feel remorse at that point was a rarity, though. Two men from the town had come through a week ago, criminals, both of them, the first to be exiled in four years. Now here was another one who was not even from the port. That situation was unheard of, as not since the six teens had any native of Caladen outside the town been exiled. The constable instructed Arden to walk beside him on the right and not to deviate from that position.

The two of them walked on a road that led them down from the walls and through several fields that gently sloped down into the town. They passed stone walls where purple and yellow flowers grew by the road. The smells of flowers and grass mixed with the subtle smell of the sea on a breeze coming up from the town.

The streets in Old Harbor were pleasant. Most of the workers lived in neat cottages with small gardens. Near the water was a large marketplace where goods were traded. The police and fire stations were up on a hill to the right of the town, overlooking the town and the water. The jail here was not as pleasant as the one in Harran, but Arden did not have to stay here as the ship was leaving that day. The constable dropped some things off at the police station, leaving Arden outside sitting on a bench, and then came out and motioned for Arden to follow.

"The other two are already on board. We need to get you there as soon as possible, for the captain wants to set sail right away," he said.

Arden and the constable walked down the main street and through the marketplace towards the docks. Arden was bombarded with the sights and sounds of the port as the last ship of the trading season was leaving. He did not have any time even to think about anything before arriving at the dock. The captain was waiting at the gangway leading to the ship. The constable turned Arden over to him and gave the captain a leather binder with papers in it. The transaction seemed very official, but the captain was laughing to himself on the inside. He had already been briefed by the king last night. He took Arden by the arm and led him on board.

"Prepare to get underway!" he yelled to the crew.

"Aye-aye, Captain," came responses from the crew all around as they got the ship ready.

"Stay close to me," the captain said to Arden, and he walked to the helm of the ship. "I'm Captain Stephens," he said to Arden, shaking his hand. "I'll introduce you to the crew and give you a tour of the ship later. For now, it would be best if you just waited over there and stayed out of everyone's way." Arden moved aside as another man came up to the captain and reported that everything was in order. "Let's get underway then, shall we?" The order was given, and slowly the boat moved away from the dock. The captain and all of the crew were dressed in white shirts and blue pants. The captain had a gold emblem on each sleeve. Several of the crew as well had different emblems signifying their positions on board. The captain was tall and strong and had a deep, commanding voice.

Arden moved closer to the side of the ship so that he could see the town as he left the shore. A crowd had gathered to watch the last ship of the season leave their shores. Arden could hear the water splashing along the side of the boat and the sails flapping as the wind caught them. All of this activity was new to Arden, who stood there almost in disbelief. As the ship got farther from the town, Arden noticed that a pier of rocks continued out from shore. He did not know that they were called breakers and that they would keep the harbor calm. The breakers were wide enough for people to walk on, and many people were on them. Some were fishing, while some younger ones were playing on the rocks, and some just seemed to be there to watch the ship, waving as it passed. At the very end of the breakers stood a man in a white robe with an open book in his hand. He was obviously a priest from the town. Next to him were a woman and three other men. As the ship approached, the crew stopped their work and gathered on Arden's side of the boat. Other men who did not seem to be part of the crew also gathered to watch alongside of him. Two other men who didn't seem to care about watching stood behind these men. As the ship left the harbor, the priest blessed the boat and crew. The blessing was solemn, and it touched Arden deeply in a way he could not understand. Later, he could not even remember what the priest had said. When his heart seemed unable to bear any more, the woman started to sing as the priest raised his hand in the final blessing. The other two men on the rocks joined in as well. Arden could not understand the words that they were singing because the language was strange.

"It is old Caladenian," said a man behind him in a slight accent. "I cannot understand it myself, but I asked the singers what it meant one time. They are singing from the Scriptures. The song speaks of men who went to sea and were tossed about and in peril on great waves. They cried out to the Lord Most High, and He delivered them. He calmed the storm and guided them safely to their destination." The man moved up next to him and said "The last part says: 'Let us give thanks to the Lord Most High for His unfailing love and wonderful deeds for men. Let the wise heed these things and consider His great love.'"

Arden watched until the singing stopped. He turned to face the man beside him. He was taller than Arden, at least at tall as the captain, but he had broader shoulders. His hair and eyes were black, and he had a beard. His kind face and friendly voice put Arden at ease. The man said, "My name is Hershel. I have been entrusted to see you safely to Jeshuryn after we arrive at Tyre. Come; let us walk to the back of the boat where you can see the town." Arden followed him to the back of the boat. The sea was calm and smooth, and Arden stood watching until the harbor faded and he could no longer tell the houses from the land. Finally, Hershel said, "Come, my son; let me show you your new home for the next two weeks."

High above the harbor, four people stood watching the ship leave from the wall: a thin girl with brown hair tossing in the breeze, a man in a black cloak behind her, and another man and woman standing together farther down the wall. As the ship left harbor, tears rolled down the girl's face from her blue eyes. The man put his hand on her shoulder, and she turned and embraced him, sobbing loudly, unable to contain herself. The man put his arms around her to comfort her. He knew that he could say nothing to help at this moment, nor should he try. Slowly, the girl's sobbing subsided, and she was able to turn and look for the ship again. It did not seem to have moved far, but she realized that it was almost out of the harbor. She left the man's embrace and walked forward to stand against the wall. The ship seemed to take forever to move, yet quickly it had moved out into the sea. The setting sun painted the sky an orange pink against the horizon. The girl watched until she could not really see the ship anymore, only the place where it had left the horizon. Tears still flowed on and off during this time. The breeze was warm and gentle. At any other time, this evening would have been beautiful. She could not hear the man behind her softly talking to himself. He did not say a word to her or act impatiently. Eventually, when she noticed the lights from the town, she realized that the night was getting dark. Just as she finally made up her mind to turn away, the man stepped forward.

"Sarah, it's time to go," he said, taking her hand. Sarah grasped the hand of the king, and they walked down from the wall together. Arden's parents remained on the wall for some time after. Sarah did not know so at the time, but she would never see the sea again.

Chapter 5

Across the Sea

Hershel gave Arden a quick tour of the ship until the evening grew dark, when they went below deck. Hershel introduced Arden to his sons. The three were traveling back to Jeshuryn on this ship, where they always sailed when they could, for the captain and crew were honest and skilful and kept the ship neat and clean. The crew were quartered aft of the passengers, using ship terms, while the captain and first mate had quarters topside near the helm. A ship's cook, navigator, and doctor were also part of the crew. The other two prisoners were quartered far aft behind the crew. Hershel scoffed at their mention but said nothing more. Hershel showed Arden his quarters: a small room with a hammock and a small table and chair. On the floor was a bucket. Arden could fit the small pack that he carried with extra clothes under the table. Arden was to stay where Hershel and his sons stayed in the passenger quarters. Arden's room was in a suite of several rooms which opened inward to a larger area with a table and chairs. Other passenger quarters stood empty, but the captain could not justify giving Arden fancy quarters. Arden said that he was not unhappy with his room and would not complain. Hershel laughed with approval. Arden could see already that this man was likeable. Hershel gave Arden some food to eat and escorted him to his cabin. He suggested that Arden get some sleep, for tomorrow would be a long day. Arden said good night and spent some time trying to get into the hammock and find a comfortable position. Eventually he fell asleep.

When he woke up the next morning, he could hear voices outside his door. He got changed and came out to where Hershel and his sons were finishing breakfast.

"Hurry and eat," they said. "We need to be up on deck soon."

Arden could feel the boat rocking with the waves, and he staggered slightly to the table. The ship was sailing to the city of Tyre and would leave its passengers there. Then the ship would sail north up the coastline and back to its own port in Nescor after making several calls on the way. Arden knew little at all about the other two Caladenian men who were prisoners being exiled to the strange lands. Only Captain Stephens knew the entire story, and he had shared it in confidence only to Hershel, whom he felt should know.

The first man, Lavin, had been a merchant in Old Harbor all of his adult life. He was an older man, tall and bald on the top of his head. He seemed normal in every way, and Arden could not see why he was banished. One day back in Old Harbor, Lavin found a small, strange bottle in a shipment of goods that had arrived. The bottle contained strong alcohol, which was forbidden in Caladen. At first, he was not sure what it was; the harsh smell burned his nose. He hid the bottle in his private office until the evening, when no one would be around. Then he tried some. It burned; so he mixed it with water and drank some more. The alcohol made him feel like he had never felt before. He was hooked. He drank it all in no time because it was such a small bottle. For the first time in his life, he was faced with a dangerous choice: to try and get more of this alcohol or to let it go. For a while, he did nothing out of fear. Then one day one of the shadier merchants from the strange lands with whom he frequently did business crossed his door. Lavin asked this man to supply him. Although the risk was great, the high price the man received was well worth it. He always brought a supply on board for the ship's crew and the other ports; so smuggling a few bottles ashore was not a difficult task. Lavin, though still fearful, waited for three days until the ship carrying the shady merchant left port before doing anything. This time, he secretly and cautiously brought the bottles home, one at a time twice a day. Then, at the end of the week, he opened the first bottle. This stuff was not as strong, and he could drink it straight. Again, the same feeling came over him, and he felt emotional and free, not like the businesslike merchant he was. But then he kept drinking and eventually got sick. His head was spinning, and he finally passed out. The next morning, he awoke when his assistant came to the door. He told his assistant that he was ill, as he certainly looked, and could not mind the store that day. The assistant did not think much of this illness and left to carry on his duty. A week later, Lavin drank again, this time forcing himself to limit the amount that he would consume.

He was able to hide his habit from everyone, but eventually it caught up with him. He began taking small bottles with him everywhere and drinking them when no one was watching. One day, he came home and drank a large amount, only to find that he had forgotten an important meeting at the church which he had to attend. He thought that nobody would notice that he was drunk, but he was wrong. He passed out and woke up in jail. He never gave up the name of his supplier, but the authorities had some idea of his identity. Lavin chose exile over prison and rehabilitation.

The next man's story was much the same. His name was Marcus, and he was a good, hard worker at the docks. One day, after unloading cargo and putting it in one of the warehouses, he found a large book at the bottom of a crate. With its brown and dusty cover, it looked like a piece of wood from a distance; so no one had noticed it. Everyone had just left for the night, and Marcus was alone when he picked up the book and opened it. To his shock, he saw that it was filled with perverse images. He closed it right away out of instinct and immediately looked around, although nobody was there. This kind of book was strictly forbidden, and before his discovery he did not even know whether such a thing really existed. His heart was telling him to get rid of it, burn it, or turn it in to the authorities. Instead, he took it home. He did not look at it that night, for he went out to eat with his fiancée and her parents. When he returned home, he was too tired to look at the book and went to bed. But in the middle of the night, he woke up and remembered it. It tormented his sleep for the rest of the night, and then in the morning he took it out and looked at it.

A week passed, and he now looked at the book every day. Evil thoughts and images were filling his mind and distracting him on the job. His fiancée and a few others noticed something different but did not know what it was. What was truly sad was that he used to come home and read the Scriptures, but now he would just look at this book instead and fantasize. A month passed before he began to seek a way to act out some of these fantasies. However, before he could, the truth was discovered when his neighbor's shed caught fire. The fire spread to the side of Marcus' house, and his bedroom window broke when the firemen sprayed water on it. The firemen and police entered his house to make sure that the fire had not spread inside the house. They did not come looking for anything inappropriate, but as they moved the bed away from the window, the book hidden behind it fell open on the floor. The constable was outraged at this book. The two firemen with him also saw it. Having witnesses of the offense, the constable took the book outside and threw it on the ashes of the shed. The book caught fire and completely burned to ashes. At the same time, Marcus came home to find a commotion around his house. A sinking feeling entered his heart, and when he opened the door, he knew his secret had been discovered. The constable arrested him on the spot. He confessed to the whole thing but did not want to seek rehabilitation or go to prison. He also chose exile instead. His fiancée was devastated by this desertion, and her heart was broken.

Although the promise of a new life in the strange lands seemed enticing, Hershel knew that it was most likely a death sentence. Life there did not have to be, but traps were waiting for travelers. During the journey to Tyre, with the captain's permission, Hershel spoke to both men one-on-one about the choices they would face. Lavin seemed to listen but did not say a word. He dismissed Hershel's warning, as he felt himself capable of succeeding in the new land. Hershel urged repentance and self-control, but Lavin, who was not listening anymore, politely left when Hershel was done. Marcus was angry and thought that Hershel was lying to perpetuate further the rule of Caladenian law over him. Marcus still was fantasizing about what he would do with his freedom. When Hershel mentioned repentance and the Lord Most High, Marcus stood up and walked out, cursing God. Hershel despaired at the men's complete disregard of their situation. Although he did his best to persuade them, seeing the indifference in them was hard. When he retired that evening, the disquiet in his heart took some time to calm.

The voyage lasted thirteen days before the crew sighted land. Each day was pretty much the same for Arden. He and the other prisoners were expected to work during the trip. Lavin helped the captain with the navigation, which Arden did not understand as it required complicated calculations to determine the ship's position. Because Lavin was not drinking, his mind was sharp, and he proved to be an asset in this endeavor. Marcus was assigned to help with the sails and any other labor that required someone strong. He was an unwilling participant in these tasks, but the captain assured him that the alternative was spending the voyage below deck in irons. Marcus agreed to help, but he only did the minimum required of him. Arden was assigned to mopping the deck, painting, and other menial tasks. His work was not intended to degrade him; he just lacked the skills for anything else that was needed. The crew kept Arden from the other two at Hershel's request, for news of another Caladenian in the strange lands would not be good for them. Hershel had no real way to avoid Arden's exposure to evil once these men fell into the hands of the queen, which Hershel suspected they would. But delaying their acquaintance as much as possible would help, for the less that they knew of Arden's situation, the better. Hershel did not know that Lavin had already heard Arden's whole story while sitting in a jail cell back in Old Harbor. The guards there did not realize that he was intently listening to everything that they said. Lavin did not really care and did not think that the information was useful.

For Arden, the journey seemed much longer than it really was. The crew and prisoners got up at dawn, had breakfast, and then went topside to do whatever task was assigned. The first two days were the worst. Much of Arden's time was spent painting. He was seasick, and the paint smell did not help. He had someone from the crew with him all of the time, really because he was a convicted prisoner from Caladen and it was the law, but the crew never told him so. They treated him well, because they could see that he tried his best in any task they gave him. In the evening, when Hershel and his sons would read the Scriptures by candlelight after the evening meal, Arden was allowed to join them. They all took turns reading, but when Hershel read, Arden felt that the words were more moving for some reason. He realized in the middle of the voyage that he was lucky to be quartered with these men. Finally, when he had begun to accept ship life, the crew sighted land mid-morning of the thirteenth day. Even though the ship had reached the coast, the captain still needed to determine their position and then make for the port of Tyre. The navigation proved to be accurate, and the port lay slightly to the north. The ship would most likely make the port by late afternoon. Arden found himself staring at the coastline of the strange lands. It did not really look any different from Caladen from this vantage point. He started to get a nervous excitement as he realized that tonight or tomorrow he would be travelling in the strange lands, the last place anyone from Caladen would want to go.

When Hershel saw the coastline, he felt conflicting emotions. Normally, his sea voyages were relaxing, and he enjoyed them. Now the responsibility of taking Arden with him weighed on his mind, more so because of the other two prisoners. He thought of a woman named Cali and his niece Ariana. He looked up at the bright stars in the sky, and they brought him some peace. He said a brief prayer for Ariana as he stargazed, not knowing that she was staring at the same stars right now and thinking of him.

Chapter 6

The Princess Ariana of Jeshuryn

The Princess Ariana was the youngest of five children. Her older siblings were, in order, an older brother Saul, a sister Shyna, a brother Jeremiah, and another brother Caleb. Being the youngest had its advantages, she thought, especially when your oldest sibling is ten years older than you. The youngest can get lost in the shuffle sometimes, becoming the most or least spoiled. Ariana was a little spoiled at first but lost that fault in her teens. Her brother Caleb was two years older, and he was closest to her of the siblings. This closeness grew partly because Caleb was very adventurous, and whenever he would try something new, Ariana would follow him. Caleb's company led to Ariana being more of a tomboy then her older sister, much more in fact. Shyna would never have played in the dirt or climbed hills in a mock battle with phantom enemies.

The land of Jeshuryn was a series of fertile plains surrounded by a ring of mountains. In the center of the kingdom, another set of mountains rose up from the plains. At the top of these mountains was the City Of Light, home to the King of Kings. At the southern base of the mountains outside the City of Light stood the mighty fortress and city of Arkadelphia. The only people that regularly entered and exited the City of Light were the messengers of the King of Kings. However, usually when a person became elderly, a messenger from the King would deliver a summons to come to the city. Receiving the summons was a time of rejoicing and sadness. Once the citizen entered the city, he would never return. Occasionally a summons would come earlier than expected. Nobody knew how that time was determined.

The only two ways into the land of Jeshuryn were at the north and south ends. In the north end, a mighty river flowed down from the mountains. Part of it ran out of the land, where the great bridge was the only crossing over the river. To the south of Jeshuryn stretched a large desert into which very few people ever ventured and out of which no outsider had come in living memory. At the southern end of the land, the mountains were not impassible, and a fortress of many walls lined the cliffs overlooking the desert. The kingdom was divided into different regions, seven in all, and each had its own ruler, or king. Above these kings was the king of Arkadelphia, and above all of them was the King of Kings. Twenty-one elders served in Arkadelphia, three for each region of Jeshuryn. Highly respected and honored, they were masters of the Scriptures in wisdom, knowledge, and practice. They would travel throughout the land, teaching, praying, and guiding the people.

When Ariana was younger, almost every year she would stay with her aunt and uncle up north in Kedesh in a town next to the great bridge. Their daughter, her cousin Sariah, was about the same age, and the girls would trade rooms for two months in the summer. For relatives to exchange cousins for the summer was common practice. The families would get to know each other better, especially those at a greater distance. In this case, getting to the distant mountains would take a week of travel. Ariana's family lived in the south in Kiriatha, while her aunt and uncle lived in the north. The families (or a portion) would meet halfway. Then, reaching the destination would take another couple of days. At the end of the summer, the villages somewhere halfway between the north and south would hold a festival where all of the families would come together and celebrate for two days.

Ariana loved staying with her Uncle Hershel and Aunt Miriam, especially because Sariah was the only child living with them. Hershel and Miriam had four older sons who were all married and out of the house. Ariana would be the only child for a change, and hence somewhat spoiled and the center of attention. Her uncle and aunt owned a store in the village which traded in all kinds of goods. Her uncle would be away sometimes for months at a time. But he always tried to be home during midsummer whenever possible. Ariana and Sariah both loved things about each others' room. Ariana loved her cousin's bed. It was very fancy-looking and had a canopy above it. Sariah's room, which was on the second floor, also had a little balcony where Ariana could look at the stars. The girls would always leave special gifts for each other. Caleb would always make fun of this custom, calling it a bribe to make sure that the girls took care of each other's room. He was really just disappointed in losing Ariana for these summer months. Sariah was not as outgoing as Ariana; so she did not spend a lot of time with Caleb. Shyna would usually baby Sariah and do girl things with her that did not interest Caleb.

Ariana was twelve years old when she went, this time, to the house of her aunt and uncle. However, this time she did not see Sariah at the halfway point, as she arrived late. The journey was meant to be that way, but Sariah did not know that. One of Ariana's aunts told her that Sariah desperately wanted to talk to her but would not say why, only that she needed to know something. These unusual incidents made Ariana very curious. When she finally arrived at her aunt and uncle's house, her relatives were just getting home from the store. They entered the house, and before a word could be said, Ariana ran straight upstairs to Sariah's room. To her utter shock, the room was completely different. Ariana found a smaller bed and a large table and chair against the wall by the door. Even more shocking was the woman who came in from the balcony when she heard Ariana enter.

"Hello," she said and smiled, "You must be Ariana. My name is Cali."

Cali apologized for taking Ariana's room and showed her where Sariah's new room was. The large canopy bed was still there, and the room was pretty much like the old one, except without a balcony. In one wall was a window with a bench in front of it where you could sit and look outside. Ariana saw a small note on the desk with her name on it, but she did not have time to open it before she was called downstairs for the evening meal. Ariana was still in disarray after the long trip and its end, and although the room change was not really such a big deal, she did notice that no gift lay on the desk as was the tradition. This omission disappointed her. However, once her Aunt Miriam and Uncle Hershel embraced her with joy and welcomed her as they always did, she felt better. They all sat down to the evening meal, which also made her forget the room because she was hungry and the food was delicious. She was still fascinated by this woman Cali who was now living at her relatives' house as part of the family, yet clearly not related. That Cali was a foreigner was very obvious because of her fair complexion. Ariana was dying to ask questions, but she knew that an interrogation so soon would be rude. She was thinking about how she could broach the subject when her aunt said, "I see you have met Cali already. She lives with us and works for us. She is an excellent seamstress and she makes the most beautiful jewelry." Cali blushed slightly at the compliment but said nothing. Ariana felt let down because she knew there had to be more to the story. Again she thought about asking questions, but she didn't, mostly because she barely had time to get in a word of her own. Her aunt and uncle were asking many questions: how is this person, how is that person, how was the trip, and so on.

By the time the meal ended, Ariana was tired, not just from eating a good meal but from the long day. Cali and Miriam went into the kitchen to clean up. Uncle Hershel brought Ariana's things upstairs and put them in the room. He said to her, "I know you have questions about Cali, but they will wait until tomorrow. Sariah left you a letter. You should read it before you go to bed. Your aunt will check on you in a while to see if you need anything. Good night, my dear." He hugged her and kissed her on the forehead. Ariana felt her eyes wanting to close, but the letter gave her some excitement and one last surge of energy. Ariana tore it open eagerly.

"My dearest Ari,

"A lot has happened this past year. I hope you don't mind the new room; I gave Cali my room. She is special, and I know you will love her like I do. I did not leave you a present, but, of course, you are getting one! It is a surprise. You will find out before we see each other again."

The rest of the letter was about things that happened in the past two years and where to find this and that in her room. It was signed, "Love Sari".

When Miriam finally came upstairs, Ariana was sound asleep on the bed. Miriam smiled and covered her niece with a light sheet. Normally, Miriam and Hershel sat outside after the evening meal and talked. Sometimes either the neighbors came over or they went over there. But because she and her husband woke at first light, they did not stay up late. Cali was not usually up at first light, but she did not sleep long past sunrise. Even now, she still had a hard time adjusting, because she found her mind often wandering and thinking at and after sunset. She usually lit a small lamp on her desk, sat on the balcony, and looked at the stars. Sometimes the sound of laughter would rise from the courtyard at the front of the house. She would sometimes hear voices but not loud enough to understand what was being said. Tonight her mind was wandering again.

When Cali looked at Ariana, she thought about her own childhood experiences. Every year, her family went north to visit her grandparents. One time when Cali was nine, her family arrived in early spring when snow was still on the ground. Cali was a curious girl, and she was allowed to go outside to explore around her grandparents' house. Her parents and grandparents trusted her because she was a very responsible girl and never got into any trouble.

The first day she did not go far, for the adults warned her as they did every year that, unlike her home, the house here was a lot more rural. Getting lost would be easy, but being found would not. Normally, she would wander around the fields nearby, but today she followed a path that led to a nearby forest. She entered it. The day was gray and cloudy, with the sun peeking through now and then. Cali kept going even when reason was beginning to suggest she stop. *Just one more corner,* she kept telling herself. Large pine trees loomed on her left, dark woods with moss covering the fallen trees. She finally stopped and began to turn around to head back when the sun came out. Brilliant shafts of light came down through an opening in the trees to the left of her. On the ground, a shiny spot looked like a mirror had been placed there, reflecting the light. She started walking towards it without even realizing she was doing so. Then she stopped. Going off the path was not a good idea in these woods. She looked around for a landmark of some sort and saw a large, fallen tree, which seemed as good as anything, except that it was not too distinctive. So she took off the pink scarf she was wearing and tied it to a broken branch sticking up from this tree. She continued off the path, looking back several times to make sure that the scarf was still visible. As she got closer to the bright spot, she realized that an opening gaped in the trees ahead. The sun went back behind the clouds and faded. The mirror on the ground was only a circular patch of snow and ice. Cali decided to explore this strange clearing. The snow was about a foot deep, and walking in it was fun. When she got near the center, the snow got deeper. Right before the very center, the snow was melted away where the sun was able to reach. In this smaller circle grew green grass, and in the very center bloomed a small, white flower. She made her way closer to look at it. Once again, the sun came out and lit the ground around her. The grass seemed a vivid, dark green, and the flower was an absolutely beautiful white lily that was so stunning to her that she just lost herself staring at it. When the sun went behind a cloud and the light faded, she was still captivated. Finally she came back to reality and realized that her back was hurting from bending in front of the lily. She sat in front of it and looked up to see if the sun was going to come out again. She waited for a while, and it finally did. Once again, she felt like she was in a patch of summer in the midst of the dark woods around this spot. She also felt at peace here. The clearing reminded her of something that her grandmother had said about the spirit of God. She could not remember the words, but she somehow felt a quiet reverence for that place. She did not want to leave it, but she knew she must. She did not really remember walking back to the path and then walking back to the house.

When she got back, she started to tell her grandmother about the peaceful clearing and the flower, but she could not find the words to explain it accurately. She often dreamed about that place and thought of it when things were not going well. It was like a private mental sanctuary where she could go when she needed to rest. Her grandparents both passed away when she was thirteen. She still felt sorrow at their passing, for now those trips were precious memories, sometimes the only good ones she thought she had left. A night bird chirped and brought her back to the present. She decided to keep her mind from wandering any further and go to bed. She extinguished the lamp and lay on the bed for a long time. She could not get the memory out of her head of her grandmother, who would sit at her bedside when she couldn't sleep and rub her back, singing gently. Like many other nights, Cali finally cried herself to sleep.

Chapter 7

Precious Stones

As Ariana settled in, she did not see much of Cali except at the evening meals. Ariana worked in the store with her aunt and spent some time with other relatives that she had not seen for some time. Cali had a small studio behind the store where she did all her work.

Aunt Miriam told Ariana that at least once a week Cali would go down to the great bridge. By the water's edge nearby she would look for precious stones for her craft. Ariana was both excited and surprised when Cali asked her to go along on the next trip. The morning came earlier than Ariana would have liked. Of course, any time earlier than when she wanted to get up she didn't like. But once awakened, she was fine. Cali and Ariana had a brief breakfast, and then they left. The day was already hot as they headed out of town; reaching the bridge took around twenty minutes.

When they reached the bridge, they saw a huge gate with towers on each side. On each side of the gate were doorways where a person could walk through. The guards seem to know Cali and greeted her. Cali introduced them to Ariana. She told them that they were going to look for stones but that first she would take Ariana to the center of the bridge. Two guards went with them, purely for the walk, as there was no danger. Ariana noticed that one of the guards had seemed really nice with Cali around. Of course, they were friendly anyway, but she guessed that this guard would not have been as friendly with anyone else. In the center of the bridge were two more towers and another gate. The towers anchored to an island in the middle of the river. On the far end were more gates. Cali and Ariana could not pass through the center gate, but the view next to it was just as good. Mountains rose up in front of them on each side of the wide and fast river. As they looked back, Cali tried to point out to Ariana where they would be walking. When they were through viewing and the guards had pointed out every landmark in sight to Ariana, the four started back. Before they made it to the gate, Ariana saw a break in the wall on the right that she had not noticed before. There, a narrow stairway led down from the bridge to the base of the tower. The guards bid Cali and Ariana good luck and returned to their posts as the ladies took to the stairs. Ariana followed Cali down a path to the right that weaved back and forth through the cliff until the two reached another path near the bottom leading away from the tower. The path led them on the cliff side away from the bridge and down towards the water. It had curved to the right, but now it curved left and brought them down below the bridge with the river in front of them.

A long shallow shore where the ladies could walk bordered an inlet from the river to the left of them. They stopped here and walked along the shore, looking for any rock or shell of interest. Cali told Ariana that when the river was high this area would be flooded and dangerous. Cali went ahead and walked out on an outcrop from the shore while Ariana walked along the shore, her feet in the water. At the end of this shore was a large tree surrounded by large rocks with flat tops where you could sit. Cali was sitting on one looking at the few things that she had gathered, throwing them back into the water. Ariana saw her as she was only three quarters of the way down and came running over with her bag. Cali tried not to laugh as Ariana emptied her bag of twenty-six rocks and one shell. Ariana was surprised that Cali had nothing.

"Are these okay?" Ariana asked.

"Place them on the rock and let them dry out. I'm afraid that they won't look as good afterwards. If you want to take a swim, this spot is a good one. But don't go out too far."

Cali had barely finished getting the words out before Ariana stripped off her clothes and jumped in the water. Ariana found the water cool and refreshing. It was deeper than she thought, too. She could not touch bottom ten feet from shore. Cali walked along the water's edge, wading up to her knees. Ariana swam by and splashed her. For a moment, she had forgotten that her companion was not another child she could play with. She expected Cali to get mad, but she just laughed. Ariana had noticed that, no matter how hot it was, Cali always wore tops that covered her arms and long pants. She did not know why and wondered if this stranger held some different moral code. But that explanation seemed strange, because Cali paid no attention to Ariana's nakedness with only the two of them there.

After a few more minutes, Cali summoned Ariana from the water. She got dressed even though she was wet - the heat would take care of drying her. She looked at the rocks she had chosen and realized that Cali was right; they were not as pretty dry as they were wet. Cali told her to keep the shell and leave the rest. The ladies walked on a path away from the water towards some small cliffs. When they got closer, a small opening appeared in the cliff before them. At the base of the cliffs was sand, like beach sand. The river was below them, and at the edge of the sand was a steep, downhill slope towards the water. Cali motioned for Ariana to join her. As Ariana got closer to the cliffs, she noticed that they glittered here and there from the sunlight. Cali led her to a spot by the cliff wall where a small wooden stool rested by several ledges. This place was obviously where Cali came to gather stones. On the ground before the pair were stones of different sizes and colors: white, yellow, red, brown, black, and green stones. A few were light blue in color. Ariana would have grabbed them all, but Cali laughed and stopped her.

"These stones are ones I've already gathered," she said. "If you walk through this opening, you'll find piles of sand and rock to look through."

"What do I look for?" asked Ariana.

"Look for small stones with even color. The most valuable stones that you can find are dark green and blue. Today we are looking for blue ones. If you see green ones or anything else you like, take it."

"Why are we looking for blue ones?"

"I am making something, and I have everything but the blue stone that I need."

They walked through the opening; the area was much bigger than it looked from the outside. Ariana chose a spot in the shade and began to dig through the sand. She resisted the temptation to grab every rock that looked good to her, and she tried to be very picky. In about an hour she was tired, and she and Cali took a break. They had carried water and some dried fruit and nuts to eat. Ariana had ten stones, and Cali had one. They laid them out on the ledge. Ariana was amazed at the one stone Cali had found. It was round like a pearl and a deep shade of green. She held it in her hand and admired it for some time.

"Will I be able to find something like this?" she asked.

"Of course you will," Cali replied. "I will show you what I look for."

"How did these stones get here?" Ariana asked.

"The stones are part of the rock in the cliffs, which crumble easily. In the winter when the water is high, this place is under water. The water wears away the rock, and the stones fall to the ground in the sand that was the rock. Sometimes I dig through the sand, and sometimes I look for places in the cliff wall where the rock is loose. I see if any stones are there and if they are loose. Sometimes I bring a small hammer and chisel to pry things loose. If I were you, I would look through the rocks over there that have recently fallen." She pointed to the spot and then got ready to resume digging.

Ariana went over to the spot and looked at the cliff wall. The wall was orange in color with veins of black stone running through it. Sometimes she could see part of the vein sparkling, and she tried to reach that spot but couldn't. She followed the vein for a while until it ran down to her height, where she saw more sparkles. Embedded in this layer were small, shiny crystals that reflected the light, making the cliffs seem to sparkle in places. But these crystals were small and not useable. She looked through the sand on the ground beneath and did not find much except the orange stone that had broken off from the wall. She was beginning to get a little discouraged because the other pile had already yielded stones by now, even if they weren't that great. But then she noticed that one of the bigger chunks of rock in front of the wall had a bluish streak next to the dark vein. This rock was as tall as she was, and the blue part ran down into the sand. Clearing away the sand, she found that the blue strip was getting wider. However, it abruptly ended where the rock had broken off from this piece. She heard Cali calling her and reluctantly went back. But Cali, calling just to make sure Ariana was okay, suggested that they take a lunch break before starting to dig. They ate some bread with cheese and some dates which Ariana had brought from the store.

After lunch, Cali walked the whole area with Ariana, looking for any obvious stones of interest. They did not find any, but Cali was not disappointed at all. They spent about an hour in one spot, digging through the sand, but did not find anything. Ariana realized that this job was not as easy as she had thought it would be. They each ended up going their own ways, and eventually Ariana came back to the same spot where she was before Cali had called her. She looked around, hoping to find the other piece of rock that would match the blue strip, which seemed to her as if it couldn't be too far away. But none of the rocks nearby were the one she was looking for. She went back to the first big rock and looked around. She had not really noticed the slight slope to the ground before, and the rock might have rolled down it. Counting on her find was reaching a bit, but she walked down the slope, where she discovered two rocks. Cali was calling again, and Ariana yelled back the "just one more minute" cry of the obsessed searcher. She grabbed the first rock, which had the very end of the streak of blue, but not crystals. She heard Cali calling her and getting closer. She knew that the second rock was her last chance for the day. The side facing up was just the orange and black cliff rock. She grabbed it and turned it over. On the other side was a thick, blue streak of rock with a pocket in the center that flashed with glittery crystals. Cali, who had finally caught up to her, looked a bit cross. But her temper was short-lived when Ariana ran to her and showed her the rock.

"Where did you find this?" Cali asked excitedly.

"Over here," said Ariana, pointing to the exact spot where the rock had lain.

"Okay, don't move," said Cali as she dropped to her knees and began to dig slowly through the sand. Ariana wasn't quite sure what Cali was looking for until she saw a fragment of blue stone. Of course, it must have been the other side of the piece she had in her hand. More fragments of blue crystal emerged, but most of them were just smooth, irregular pieces. They were valuable, but not what Cali was looking for. Then she stopped abruptly and looked down. Ariana could not see what she had found. Then Cali held up a stone: a deep blue, faceted crystal which looked dark until Cali held it up in the sunlight to reveal a bright, clear blue that shone brilliantly in the sun.

"Amazing," Cali said, unable to find any other words to say. A tear almost filled her eye, and the way she looked at Ariana made her feel like Cali had expected to find this exact stone. Cali took out a small cloth bag, put the gem inside, and carefully tied the top shut. Then she put the small bag in a larger one she carried along with the other pieces. She let Ariana carry the rock she'd found, and the two went back to where they had first entered the cliffs. Cali put a few other stones that she had found in her bag, and then she and Ariana gathered all of their belongings together and began to head back.

When the ladies had climbed up the stairs to the great bridge, the two guards that had escorted them were still at the entrance to the bridge but were ready to head back to the town. Ariana showed the guards the rocks that she had found, and they were impressed with the blue crystals. Two other guards coming down from the town joined them, and Cali showed them the one blue gem. The guards were excited at the find, and they rejoiced. Cali gave Ariana the credit, and the guards all congratulated her as she beamed with pride.

Just then, everyone turned at the sound of a horse coming across the bridge. The center gate on the near side opened, and a rider came through.

A guard from the center entrance shouted, "Make way for a messenger of the King of Kings!"

Seeing messengers of the King of Kings traveling throughout the land was not that uncommon. Ariana had never seen one coming across the great bridge, and she had not beheld one so close before. He rode towards them on a large, dark brown horse wearing the typical red shirt with gold symbols on it. He had taken off his helmet at the gate, giving Ariana a better view of his appearance. She did not really know what to expect, for messengers did not seem to mingle with the people, who looked upon them with a sense of awe and reverence. This messenger had short, black hair and a tired look on his face.

The guards hailed him and welcomed him back to Jeshuryn.

To Ariana's surprise, he smiled as he said, "It is good to be home again." For some reason, she had expected him to be stern and not really friendly, but she was wrong.

The guard that liked Cali said, "We are escorting these ladies back to town, and we would be honored if you would accompany us, if we would not slow you down."

The messenger replied, "I will gladly join you. My business has taken me far, and to spend a short time with such fair people would do my heart well."

The party set off towards the town. As they walked, the guards told the messenger of the find that the ladies had made. Even though the horse was only going at a walk, Ariana could not keep up with it or the adults; so the messenger stopped to let her catch up.

"Let the child ride with me," he said. So two guards lifted Ariana up, and she sat in front of the messenger. She held the rock in front of her on her lap as they walked towards the village.

"May I see this rock of yours?" he asked.

"Of course," she said, handing it to him, and he studied it carefully for a moment.

"It is very nice," he said, and he gave it back to her. She noticed that he was wearing a ring of gold on his hand. His pants and boots were dusty from the road, but the travel stain did not diminish his authoritative appearance.

The messenger said nothing of his business beyond the bridge, and the guards did not ask. Ariana wanted to ask but did not. The group talked about the weather and the crops and other things that did not really interest Ariana. So she started to imagine herself as a princess returning home from a heroic battle with victorious forces. She pictured Caleb riding his horse alongside of her and imagined the great celebration waiting for them when they returned home. She thought of her father and mother greeting the victors warmly and the other siblings impressed by their triumph. The people loudly cheered for the conquerors by name.

As the group approached the town, others who saw them coming also went out to join them. Soon, a whole group of people had entered the town center and gathered outside the store of Hershel and Miriam. When Ariana's aunt and uncle heard the joyous voices of the crowd outside, they also went out to join them. For one second, Miriam's heart stopped when she saw Ariana on the horse with the messenger, for she thought that he had come for her. But he handed her down and then dismounted. Ariana ran to her aunt and showed her the rock. Hershel was surprised to see Ariana on the horse as well, but only because riding one was a great honor seldom conferred.

The messenger took a break for refreshment. Someone took the horse to tend to it without needing to be asked. Thus was the respect and honor for these men. The townspeople asked him to stay, but he said that he had to continue as far as he could that day and that he still had plenty of light left to travel. The town bid him farewell, and he rode off down the road. The crowd dispersed, and as Ariana watched the messenger leave, the sight reminded her of a dream she once had but could not remember. The sky was dark blue, and a sweet fragrance hung in the air. She walked to the edge of the town, where she could see the road stretching out below. In the distance, she could see the small outline of the messenger as he rode through the green fields. As she gazed outwards, she realized that he was right; their land was fair and pleasant.

Later at the supper table, Hershel said, "I heard that you ladies found quite the prize stones today." Although she was not normally allowed, Ariana was able to leave the table and get her treasures to show everyone. She brought her rock with the crystal pocket and the blue fragments that they had found as well as the other rocks she gathered. "And what of the gemstone?" he asked. Then Cali took a small pouch from her pocket and shook out the stone. Hershel held it up between his finger and thumb, and it sparkled with a brilliant blue. He was very impressed by the gem. "And what will you do with it?" he asked.

"It is the last stone for a piece I am making," she said. "It is the one that I told you and Miriam about." Hershel and Miriam had not seen Cali so excited for some time.

"Ah, of course," he said, smiling, "excellent, truly excellent."

"Good, good," said Miriam, smiling too. "Praise to the Lord Most High."

Ariana was in the dark, but she was too happy about her own pieces to care. All she really wanted was the one rock with the crystals inside. The rest she had given to Cali.

"Just like that," said Hershel, laughing when Cali told him. "Well, our niece may not have much business sense, but she certainly has the heart of the Lord." Ariana did not know that even the blue fragments would become expensive pieces of jewelry at Cali's skilled hands.

"Hershel!" said Miriam in a laughing rebuke, "the heart is all that matters." She hugged Ariana and kissed her on the forehead. Ariana found that day to be the second best day of the summer.

Chapter 8

The Storm and Story

A riana and Cali had not seen much of each other in the past week. Ariana was busy in the store and still meeting distant relatives, while Cali was working constantly and seemed intent on completing something as quickly as possible. Ariana usually slept through the night, but she woke up one night and saw light coming from Cali's room. Ariana knew that the light had something to do with the blue stone that she and Cali had found, but she did not know what it was.

One night, Uncle Hershel and Aunt Miriam went out to visit friends and stay with them for the night; so after supper Cali and Ariana were on their own. After a very hot day, a coming storm promised lots of lightning and thunder. Although Ariana would not completely admit it, she was frightened of storms like that. Distant thunder sounded during supper, although the sky above was still blue and the sun was out. When Ariana was clearing the table and had gone into the kitchen, Aunt Miriam quietly asked Cali to stay with Ariana until bedtime, because of Ariana's fear. Cali would usually go to her room alone, but tonight she invited Ariana to sit with her outside on the balcony.

So after Ariana and Cali finished cleaning up after supper, they went upstairs and sat together on the balcony outside Cali's room. The sky was still clear on this side of the house, but they still heard distant thunder. Cali sat holding a cup of tea, which she usually drank after supper. She looked very tired, and Ariana felt tired just looking at her. For some reason, Ariana felt herself staring at Cali while Cali was looking out at the evening sky. Ariana suddenly noticed how beautiful the older girl was, not that she had ever thought Cali unattractive, but in this moment, Ariana had an image in her mind of Cali as a beautiful and sweet child the same age as her. She wondered what Cali was like as a child. Ariana turned away and looked at the sky before Cali could notice her staring. Large, puffy clouds in the distance glowed in a pink light from the sun that was hidden from view. When Cali finished her tea, she fetched some needlework and brought it out to work on it. Ariana did not want to find an occupation, but she left and got a book to read. Saria had left her the book which contained stories from the Scriptures for younger children. It wasn't a bad book, but back on Cali's balcony, Ariana's mind was wandering. She could not concentrate; she was still thinking about Cali. One time when Cali had gone down to the bridge, Aunt Miriam told her that Cali was from the distant land of Caladen across the sea. Uncle Hershel had traveled to this land to trade almost every year. He said that the people were friendly but did not let outsiders into their land. In that sense it was like her country, and she was more surprised to learn that they believed in the Lord Most High and the King of Kings. Yet Cali never participated in the worship services at the temple. She held hands when Ariana's family prayed after the meal, but she did not say anything. Ariana pointed this silence out to her aunt and uncle, but they gently rebuked her. "It is not for us to judge her," said her uncle, "but we must continue to pray for her."

Ariana continued to think about Cali while looking out at the sky. A few of the brighter stars glowed in the deep twilight, and Cali stopped working because the night was getting too dark. She brought her needlework back inside and put it away. Ariana felt a sudden weariness and wanted to go to bed. She was mad at herself because she had wanted to stay up and spend the evening with Cali, and now she wasn't going to stay awake. She turned and found Cali looking at her.

"You look tired, and it is almost your bedtime," Cali said.

"I know," said Ariana, "but I was hoping to stay up with you."

"Why don't you go and lie down for a while? If you wake up and my light is on, you can come back in, and we can talk."

Ariana felt so much better hearing this concession that she went contentedly to her room. Within minutes, she was sound asleep. Hours later, she woke to the sound of thunder. She could hear the sound of rain outside and could smell it as the wind blew through her window. She shut the window, for the wind was increasing with the approaching storm. She got up and went out into the hall, but no light shone from Cali's room. A flash of lightning scared her, and she ran back to bed. She waited as the thunder and lightning increased, hoping to see a light from Cali's room. She knew that her aunt would have come in to check on her by now. On the other hand, she felt like kind of a baby; after all, she was twelve years old. Maybe Cali did not know how afraid she was or even think that she would be afraid. Now the storm was closer. The lightning was brighter, and the thunder was louder. Ariana had just begun to ask the Lord for help when she saw a light coming from the hallway. She wasted no time in running to Cali's room. Cali had just finished lighting the lamp on her desk and was getting a candle when Ariana came through the door (she barely kept herself from running) and threw her arms around her. Just then, another lightning and thunder combination hit, and Ariana squeezed her like she was in a wrestling match. Cali almost laughed. But Ariana was trembling, and Cali realized how frightened this child was. So Cali walked Ariana over to the bed and sat on the edge of it with Ariana in her lap, sort of. But the position was very uncomfortable; so she lay back on the bed and held Ariana next to her while the storm passed. Then the worst of it was over, and the frequency of thunder decreased as the storm moved away. Ariana was relieved but felt a bit embarrassed. She sat up and apologized for being such a baby. Cali laughed and reassured her that it was all right. She told Ariana that she could stay for a while until the storm passed, but Ariana said that she was all set. Cali walked Ariana back to her room, and she went back into bed. Cali said good night and left.

Ariana lay there for a few minutes and felt like she should have thanked Cali more for comforting her. Part of her said "do it tomorrow," but she decided to get up and do it now, as Cali's light was still on. Ariana went out into the hallway and straight into Cali's room. Before she could even say anything, she stopped. Cali had taken off her robe and stood with her back to the door. Ariana had never seen Cali without long sleeves or any of her back exposed, and now she knew why. She must have gasped, and Cali heard her and turned around.

"I just … came to say thank you," she said, bursting into tears.

Cali felt a surge of anger at the intrusion but then realized it was too late. Ariana's tears changed her heart completely. "Come here," she said, "you can look."

Cali sat down sideways on the chair in front of the desk with her back facing the light. Ariana came closer and looked. Cali's back was covered with long scars from top to bottom.

Her left arm had one long scar from the top down to her wrist in a twisting pattern. Her right arm looked normal except for the scars completely around her wrist.

"Do … they … hurt?" Ariana asked.

"No," said Cali. "Not for a long time. You can touch them if you want."

Ariana found herself running her fingers up Cali's arm. The scars felt smooth and strange to her touch. She gingerly touched Cali's back. The scars were like furrows where something had cut deeply into the flesh. Ariana saw tears in the corners of Cali's eyes and wondered if she had hurt her.

"I'm sorry," she said.

"It's not your fault," Cali said, and then "you're not hurting me. It is a deeper hurt."

Ariana did not know what to say at this point. To Cali's surprise, the girl sat on her lap and began to cry. Cali embraced her and felt hot tears running down her back. Maybe Cali had expected Ariana to run away in fear; she never had expected this reaction. Cali felt something happening in her heart, but she did not know at first what it was. Then she realized the love she felt for this child. This revelation was exactly as the angel had told her. Although she already knew so in her heart, this love confirmed that Ariana was the one.

Cali knew that Ariana would never ask, could never ask, what had happened. She also knew that she could never fully explain to this child what had happened in a way that she could understand. And that barrier of innocence was not a bad thing. So Cali took Ariana, wiped the tears from her eyes, kissed her on the forehead, and sat her on the bed. Cali put her robe back on and rearranged the pillows on the bed so that the two of them could sit together. Ariana lay with her head in Cali's lap as Cali told her the story. She did not tell it all, even though it was all in her mind.

Cali was one of the six teens who were banished from Caladen when they had refused to take the oath of allegiance to the Lord Most High. She barely remembered the sea voyage except that she got seasick the first part of the journey. She also remembered feeling sad deep inside, but she refused to acknowledge or admit her grief to her friends. She was so in love with Rya that she knew everything would be fine as long as they were together. Eventually, both the seasickness and the homesickness passed, and the teens arrived at the port of Tyre.

When the six arrived in the port of Tyre, Cali didn't even wonder at the time that an envoy from the Queen met them at the docks and invited them to the palace. She remembered how excited she was then. The six traveled to the city of Ashkelon, where the Queen welcomed them in person and invited them to be part of her court. Cali and the others were thrilled. Immediately they were given quarters, three rooms in the great palace at their disposal. The pairing was obvious: Cali and Rya, Mari and Jon, Kayla and Trent. Plenty of food and drink abounded. The newcomers were excited about the drinks, because alcohol was forbidden in Caladen. The Queen had parties almost every night, some large and some small. The absence of the Queen's parties didn't matter, because the young people would party together anyway, with or without the Queen. One day every month or so would be the Queen's festival day, a large gathering of all Queen's court and guests and envoys from other lands. The festival started with feasting and drinking at noon. The first time Cali went, the celebration was much larger than she imagined. With so many people, the six teens became separated. Cali met two girls, a girl her age named May and an older girl named Liva. May, who was kind and made Cali feel at ease, had been at the palace for five months since she had come from the city of Tyre. Liva had been there for four years and, although she seemed pleasant enough, Cali felt a dislike for her and thought her pleasantness was phony. She wanted to get away from her as soon as possible, and with seeming luck, Liva left to go check out the "new talent," as she put it. Cali suspected what she meant, but the thought got lost in her mind as May took her by the hand and led her away. Time seemed to fly by, and before Cali knew it, the day started to wane. May had introduced her to many people who were all charming with great stories to tell. Cali did not even notice or care that nobody wanted to know her or her story. When the evening started to get dark, May took Cali back to her room to get changed for the evening. Cali was glad, because her head was spinning from the drinks. May said that she was glad to share her clothes and that, as she and Cali were about the same size, she would find something for her to wear. While Cali sat with her head on the table, May went into another room and changed. When she came out, Cali was stunned. She looked so much older, and her outfit was very sexy. May was wearing makeup that totally covered her face, and although many would call her beautiful, the paint made her look less pretty to Cali. May saw Cali's discomfort from the alcohol and gave her a leaf to chew. The effects were quick; Cali felt awake and alert. May had picked out an outfit for Cali, a bright red dress that was just as revealing as hers. May put makeup on Cali's face, and when she was through, she dragged her to the mirror laughing. Cali was just as shocked to see herself transformed into this new person. She laughed to herself and couldn't wait until the others saw her, especially Rya.

When the girls left the room, they were slightly late getting to the main hall, which was quiet because the Queen was speaking, welcoming everyone. They were handed a small cup with red liquid inside. May warned her not to drink it until the Queen commanded. Cali agreed, but her mind was not really present. She was totally lost looking at the crowd of people, who had all changed into different clothes. May was holding her hand and guiding her through the crowd to get closer to some boys that she knew. She said something about being in the right spot at the right time, but Cali didn't hear. Finally, after several laughs from the crowd and cheers of approval, the Queen bid everyone to drink. Cali emptied her cup without a second thought. She felt an explosion of warmth in her body accompanied by a surge of sexual energy that she did not know was possible. What happened next cannot be told, but can be inferred for sure. Cali wanted to find Rya, but when she did, he was with Liva. Cali felt almost like Liva was waiting for this moment. She gave Cali a look that was a combination of a smirk and a glare of contempt. Cali turned away and resumed what she was doing with others.

The next morning, or afternoon to be more accurate, she woke up with a splitting headache. Rya was in bed next to her. She remembered that she had found Rya somewhere in the night, and despite what he had done, they got together and somehow reached their room. After all, she was just as guilty as he was. As more and more memories of the night before gripped her, she ran to the toilet to vomit. Later that day, the six met together. Mari and Kayla told Cali how much fun they had and what a great night they had spent. Their opinion seemed to be the general consensus. Cali wondered if she had missed something. She drank again that night in a vain attempt to forget the festival. She came to understand much later that this revel was the beginning of the end. Strangely enough, she never saw Liva again.

Six years passed. Cali and Rya still lived together but hardly spoke when they were together. They were no longer the friends they had once been. Everything had changed. Cali often went to see May and would stay with her. Sometimes Cali would go to May's room just to get away from Rya. Occasionally, she would stay with other guys just like Rya would stay with other girls, even though they would never openly admit this unfaithfulness to each other. May had changed, but she was always kind to Cali. She loved to gossip and was the source of information to the Queen about the happenings of the city, though nobody but she and the Queen knew of her usefulness. May's spying and gossip had guaranteed the success of her father in Tyre, and May knew that she would be leaving soon to return to Tyre as the bride of the city ruler. Cali did not care about the gossip of the land, but May would always tell her anyway. Cali, who hoped that May would somehow be able to take her with her, did not know how to ask. She wasn't sure that this change of location would even help, but it would get her out of the queen's city. She had found work making jewelry for many of the new girls that came to the palace and she could also sew very well. She hoped that May would realize how skilled she was and want her to go with her.

Sometimes, Cali saw herself back in the forest in the clearing with the white flower. Sometimes she dreamed about the clearing. But each time, the dark forest would become darker, closing menacingly around her. One night after drinking too much, she fell asleep in May's room when May was away. Cali found herself sitting on a stone in the middle of the bright patch of white snow. She felt the warm sun on her face and looked down to find that she was dressed in a gown of white. But when she looked outside the circle, thorn bushes surrounded her, and the dark forest seemed shrouded in night, even though the sun was shining. She realized that thorns and darkness completely surrounded the circle. The sight of the lowering hedge made her despair, and she felt a sense of panic rising deep within her. Then she became aware of a hand on her shoulder. The touch was gentle and peaceful, and it made her forget about the darkness. As the brightness increased around her, she thought she could hear someone speaking, but the voice was so far away that she could not understand it, if it was a voice at all. She tried to turn around and see who was speaking, but she was frozen and unable to move. Finally, when she started to turn around, she woke up. She went to May's window and stood there, looking out over the city. Lights burned all through the city, and loud voices and raucous laughter echoed now and again. As Cali stood there, she felt something she had not felt in a long time, a feeling of loss and regret, like when her grandparents passed away. Tears streamed down her face. She thought about jumping out the window, wondering if the fall below would kill her, until something inside overrode those thoughts, and the peace she had felt in the dream came back for a moment. She turned away from the window and saw the almost empty bottle on the table, and she hated it, hated what she had become. But she drank the rest of it anyway and went back to bed.

Cali had recently realized that greed and lust drove almost everyone in the palace – just like her. And the more that they all fulfilled that lust, the harder it was to satisfy. Their lust was a trap that they could never escape. She saw how Rya and the other guys couldn't wait until new girls arrived. Even the other two girls from Caladen couldn't stop talking about the new guys in the palace guard. Cali saw a new girl at the festival and instantly hated her. This girl was loud and had drunk too much, and a crowd of guys surrounded her. Cali noticed that one guy among them didn't seem to laugh as hard as the others, and although he covered his discomfort well, she could see that this was the loud girl's boyfriend and that they must have just come into the palace together. She felt sorry for him for one second before she wanted to seduce him just to hurt the other girl. Then she remembered Liva. That memory almost brought her to her senses, but she had another drink instead.

Cali never knew it, but the day before this festival the Queen had summoned Rya to her chambers. She wanted to get rid of Cali, preferably by killing her, but without losing Rya. She was grooming him to be one of the overseers of the city finances, and he was doing a great job.

"I have just too many girls in the Queen's court," she said, sighing.

"I heard that May is leaving soon," Rya replied.

"Yes, but it would be nice if some of the older girls could go. I don't mean to get personal, but you and Cali don't seem to getting along very well." After a moment, she said with seeming sympathy, "It's just that I hate to see you unhappy. You and Brea seem like you would make a good couple."

Rya said, "Please don't think any less of me, my Lady, but I would prefer it if Cali left. Yet I don't want her killed."

"Please," the Queen said as she recoiled in feigned horror, "I would never do that. What would you have us do?"

"Sell her as a slave," said Rya.

The next morning, Cali had made up her mind to ask May if she could go with her. She was debating whether she would even say anything to Rya or just leave. She was surprised when guards came and summoned her to the Queen's court. A sick feeling entered her stomach, but she could not refuse the summons. When she arrived, only the queen and a cruel-looking man in a black robe were in the room.

"Will she do?" asked the Queen.

"Yes, your majesty," said the man with a sly smile.

"What is the meaning of this?" asked Cali.

The Queen laughed loudly and said, "The meaning, my dear, is that now is the time for you to leave us. And what better way could you find, friendless exile that you are, than to be sold as a slave? Meet your new master, Ali Had-Assan."

Cali was shocked. "What? ... You can't do this!" Then the guards grabbed her and bound her hands behind her back. Outraged, she shouted a stream of obscenities at the Queen.

"Take her away!" said the Queen.

The guards dragged her out and lifted her up onto a waiting horse. They tied her hands and feet so that she could not dismount. Her new master rode out on his horse, leading her horse away with him. They rode north out of the city towards the wilderness between the cities. Now, Ali was an evil man who had no intention of keeping Cali alive any longer than the trip home to his city, which was five days away. He would never be allowed to keep a female slave like her, much less a foreigner, without his father's permission, which that man wasn't likely to give. So Cali's temporary master planned on having his sport with this girl and then killing her. The Queen knew of this plan and had approved; the knowledge of Cali's torture and death made the price of her sale even sweeter. However, Ali had the misfortune to ride right into another group of his fellow citizens also heading for home. They were stopping in the nearby city to the west, and they urged Ali to come with them. He could not refuse, and he cursed the queen in front of them for making him take this evil whore with him. So he and his countrymen rode through the afternoon until they reached the city of Meclah. Now Cali was given nothing to eat or drink this whole time, and she was emotionally sick at heart as well.

When the travelers arrived at the city, they found a special group of houses that were set aside for the other travelers, and Ali was forced to go with them. The houses were arranged like a small town surrounding a central courtyard. A large house where the important leaders would stay stood on one side. The travelers rode into the courtyard and dismounted. Ali untied Cali's feet and pulled her down from the horse. She landed hard on the ground, and he dragged her kicking to a small fountain and statue, where he tied her. Because Ali could not tell the truth of his intentions, he just said that this woman was now a slave. The other women in the party of travelers came over and looked at her with disgust. An older woman ripped the shirt off of her, revealing the tattoos going up her left arm and around her right wrist. Because tattoos were forbidden, Ali feigned outrage and said that he did not know about them. The old woman spit on Cali and walked away to some evil purpose. Ali grabbed a whip and ordered

Cali to be tied to a whipping post. Cali was crying and afraid. Ali gave her ten brutal lashes, even though she passed out from the first two. The men stood around and laughed. As if this pain wasn't enough, the old woman had gone to get some irons from the fire to burn the tattoos off. Cali woke up from the searing pain and screamed as the woman burned her skin.

Unknown to all of these men, the ruler of their homeland, Ali's father, was inside the big house. He was at that moment concluding an important agreement with a merchant named Hershel from Jeshuryn. The ruler was not a cruel man, like his youngest son outside, but a wise one. The trade deal that he and Hershel were making was very profitable to both sides, and he was pleased. He and his guest barely heard the sound of men arriving outside. Then they thought that they heard two loud screams. Hershel's son Jorham along with the right-hand man of the ruler went to see what was happening. A few minutes later, Jorham came back and, bowing first to the ruler and asking forgiveness for the intrusion, said, "Father, come quickly." The right-hand man of the ruler also returned and whispered in the ear of the ruler. The ruler and Hershel got up and headed for the outer balcony. As they approached, they heard screaming. They reached the balcony as the woman, half surrounded by cheering men, was burning Cali's wrist.

"What in the name of all that is holy...?" said Hershel.

Before Hershel could even protest, the ruler shouted "Stop!" at the top of his voice, which echoed through the courtyard. All eyes turned to the balcony. The men's hearts were filled with fear, and they dropped to their knees. The woman dropped the iron and fell to her knees as well. The courtyard was silent except for the sound of Cali sobbing.

The ruler was furious. Ironically, he had just finished explaining to Hershel that his people had given up the barbaric ways of their past. At the sound of his voice, guards came running into the courtyard and onto the balcony. The ruler shouted orders at them, and they seized his son Ali and the old woman and beheaded them right in front of Cali, who passed out at the sight. The other men were herded at sword point into a small enclosed garden at the left of the courtyard. The ruler apologized most sincerely to Hershel. Hershel went down to the courtyard to see the girl. As he cut her bonds, she collapsed in shock and pain. "Who is this girl?" he asked. The ruler demanded the guards to get an answer immediately. They came back and said that she was just sold as a slave from the queen's city.

"What will happen to her?" Hershel asked, knowing full well that she would not be any more welcome in this brutal country now than she had been before, especially after embarrassing the ruler.

The ruler in his wisdom said, "Please take her and tend to her. I will pay any expense that you incur."

So Hershel and his sons took Cali with them back to Jeshuryn. She did not remember the journey, for she was feverish and weak. When Hershel's party arrived at the great bridge, they found that a messenger from the City of Light had already been sent with the word to let Cali enter the land. So Hershel and Miriam took her into their house and tended to her. The elders came and prayed for her, and the fever left but the wounds took many days before they would heal. Miriam washed and dressed them daily, and Sariah helped where she could.

Eventually, when Cali was strong enough to stand on her own, she would walk down to the great bridge with Sariah to look out over the water, which seemed to bring her some peace. She did not know what would happen to her, and she considered herself a slave now owned by Hershel and Miriam. When she said so, they protested, shocked, because they could not own any other person. They told Cali that she was free to leave but that she was also welcome to stay in their house. As Cali had nowhere to go, she stayed. Miriam helped her find clothes that she could wear and learned of Cali's talent as a seamstress. Then she learned that Cali also had tremendous talent at making jewelry. The women of Jeshuryn did not wear overwhelming, gaudy jewelry like the women in the queen's city but tasteful and beautiful jewelry for the appropriate situations. So Cali adapted her style to make quality pieces rather than quantity. She looked at Hershel and Miriam like her grandparents, because they reminded her of them.

When she finished telling the abridged story, Cali walked Ariana back to her room and put her to bed. Ariana was greatly distressed by Cali's history because of the many things in it that she did not understand. She told Cali that the King of Kings would forgive her for any of the bad things she had done. However, tiredness overtook her, and she was soon fast asleep. By now the storm was over, and the stars shone above. Back in her own room, Cali sat on her balcony for a while. The seven stars glittered brightly tonight. She recalled the vision that had appeared to her. One day while she was looking for stones, a man dressed in white suddenly emerged from thin air. Cali was afraid, but he told her not to be. He told her that she must make a pendant with the seven stars, and he put the image of it in her mind. "You must give it to a young girl who is a princess in the land. You will know the one of whom I speak when you feel a great love for her in your heart." Cali had shared this vision with Miriam and Hershel, and they agreed that her visitor was an angel from the Lord Most High. Tonight, Cali just stared at the stars for some time. She tried to think about how vast the heavens must be and how small she was. It was some time before she could relax and finally get some sleep.

Chapter 9

The Festival

The summer passed by quicker than Ariana would have liked, and before she knew it, the End of Summer Festival was two weeks away. The good news was that it would take place here in Kedesh. Soon, two weeks became a week, and then a week became three days. Preparations had already begun, including a huge tent pavilion filled with tables and benches inside where people would eat. The tent had been erected on a field right outside the town, and another large tent stood next to it where the food would be kept. The townspeople were also preparing the town center for the evening events. Everyone would gather together there in their best clothes after the sun had set for a solemn moment of prayer and a short service honoring the King of Kings and the Lord Most High. Afterwards, a time of celebration and dancing would run until midnight. After the last dance, everyone would join hands to sing a traditional song and then end the evening in prayer. Even now, families had started to arrive, some coming back home and others attending the festival. Despite the excitement around her, Ariana was more worried about what she was going to wear, because she had not brought anything with her that was appropriate for the dance. Her aunt laughed when she expressed this fear and assured her that her wardrobe would be a priority.

Meanwhile, Cali found herself walking down to the river and heading for the place where she looked for stones. Her journey was pointless, because nothing that she wanted was there; she just needed to get away from the busyness of the preparations. Something was bothering her deep inside, and she could not understand what it was. The more she pondered, the more the source of her agitation eluded her. Then a realization hit her; the families coming together poked at her spirit like a burr in a hem. Somewhere long ago in her childhood, she recalled a similar gathering that happened every year. One year, it was at her house, and she remembered playing outside with her cousin Mary. They were ten years old, and they both were dreaming about the future and everything that they would have: a husband, house, children, garden, horse, etc. They teased each other about the future husbands. Cali did not even know Rya then. Out of everything that they had dreamed and wanted, Cali never got any of it, and now it was too late. Something about that loss made her cry hard, lamenting the things that she had never had, especially children. She cried for quite a while in this mental world of emptiness until she came back to the present, lying on the ground in the sand under the hot sun. She stumbled back to the place by the water's edge where she and Ariana had gathered shells and sat on the large rock there. Her hair had sand in it, and she took a short swim in the water to rinse it out. The cool water was refreshing, and she sat on the rock for sometime afterward in the shade. She felt oddly free now and almost emotionless, cool and clear headed. She took a few deep breaths and walked back to the town. Ariana saw her approaching and ran up to her, embracing her. Cali embraced her back, finding that she could just love Ariana without thinking of anything else.

As they walked back, Ariana asked Cali what she was going to wear to the dance. Cali told her that she did not plan on attending and went back to her work. When Ariana told her aunt, Miriam was distressed. She went to Cali and told her that she was welcome and that her absence would be a dishonor to their family. When Cali heard that her adopted family would suffer, she agreed to go without hesitating. That cooperation surprised Miriam, but she was pleased and told Ariana that Cali would attend. That evening, Hershel did not eat with the family, for he was helping with the preparations. Tonight was the perfect time for Ariana to receive the first gift. Miriam and Cali went to Cali's room, and they called Ariana in.

"So, you're worried about what you're going to wear for the dance," laughed Miriam. "Well, we have a surprise for you. I think Sariah told you about it in her letter."

At that moment, Cali brought out a dress that she had made for Ariana. It was made of black material hemmed with gold fabric in an intricate pattern. Ariana was very surprised and excited.

"Can I try it on?" she asked.

"Of course," said Cali. "I need you to put it on so that I can make alterations if necessary."

"Sariah has a matching dress as well," said Miriam. "This dress is her gift for you."

Ariana tried it on to find that very few alterations needed to be made. During this time, Hershel came home. He could hear the ladies talking and laughing upstairs; so he decided to remain downstairs. Eventually, the ladies came downstairs, and Ariana modeled the dress for her uncle. He gave his approval and spun her around, pretending that they were dancing.

Ariana suddenly asked, "What about you, Cali? What are you going to wear?"

"I don't know," said Cali sadly. "I do not have anything that would be appropriate for the dance."

"And that is where you are wrong," said Miriam. She motioned to Hershel, and he left the room and came back with a long cloth bag, which he laid on the table. "Well, open it," said Miriam. "This is our surprise for you."

Cali, speechless, slowly opened the bag and removed a long, white dress made of expensive fabric. Ariana was glued to her side as she was taking it out.

"It's beautiful. Try it on! Please," said Ariana.

Cali's eyes were starting to well with tears. "We'll be back," said Miriam, and the ladies went upstairs again. Hershel sighed. Cali put on the dress, and it fit perfectly. The sleeves were long, and the skirt was ankle length. The fabric was a soft, white material. Around the neck were interwoven threads of blue, green, and gold. Subtle patterns ran through the sleeves and the hem. The dress was elegant and completely appropriate for the festival. Cali was still wondering how this perfectly fitted, elegant dress could be, and Miriam laughed. "You are not the only seamstress in the land, my dear. I was able to measure your clothes when you were down at the river." Cali hugged her and cried. Ariana was bursting with joy. Once again, the ladies went downstairs, and Cali thanked Hershel. Hershel just praised the Lord for providing.

"Now, we have one more surprise, if we can handle one more," he laughed. "It is for you, Ariana." He left the room and returned with a small, wooden box. Opening the box, he removed a pendant from inside. As Hershel held it up, Ariana could see that it had seven stones in the same pattern as the seven starts in the sky. The center stone was the bright blue one that Cali had found with Ariana. Hershel handed it to his niece, and she gingerly took it in her hands. Hershel explained that this pendant was not just another piece of jewelry and that Cali had a visit from an angel who told her to make it. "There is one catch, however," he said, and both Miriam and Cali were surprised when he said: "you cannot wear it to the dance."

"Why?" asked Miriam.

Hershel explained. "I was sitting by the gate outside the town, taking a short rest after helping set up the pavilions, when suddenly a man was standing before me. He greeted me in the name of the Lord Most High and asked if the pendant was ready. I told him it was and did not even think it strange that he would ask such a question.

"He said, 'You may show the pendant to Ariana, but she cannot take possession of it until her eighteenth birthday. You must give it to her father for safekeeping until then. When she takes possession of it, she must wear it at all times, but it must remain hidden. The King of Kings will tell her when she may wear it openly. Do you understand these instructions?

"'Yes,' I replied.

"The stranger said, 'That is good. Do not speak of this matter to anyone until you present the pendant to Ariana. Peace be to you, Hershel; the Lord Most High is pleased with you and has blessed you and prospered you.

"I bowed my head at this time, and when he finished speaking, I looked up to find that he was gone. I tried to stand up; instead, I woke up and realized that I had seen a vision from the Lord Most High. So we must do what we are commanded."

Ariana was disappointed, and Cali was a little confused at this restriction. But none of those present could doubt that this vision was a message from the Lord Most High. Cali realized that, because her family believed her story about her vision, she had to believe this message.

Seeing the look on the faces around him, Hershel said, "I am just as surprised as you are. However, we must trust and believe that the Lord Most High has a reason for these instructions."

"Of course," said Miriam.

They all looked at the pendant one last time, passing it from person to person. The mood was solemn now. Ariana, the last to hold the pendant, put in gently into the box. *Someday I'm going to meet the King of Kings* she pondered to herself.

The festival day seemed to go by way too fast for Ariana. She spent the morning helping her aunt and others prepare the food. As the people were assembling around the tent, Ariana heard the sounds of laughter and kids playing. Some musicians were playing, and now and then someone would sing a song. Ariana saw her older sister and brothers and ran to greet them. Soon everyone had arrived, including her parents, who were some of the last people to come, along with the king of Kedesh. Ariana had planned to sit with Sariah and Cali but could not find either one. She ended up sitting between her mother and father. At first, being in the center of the tent with the king of Kedesh and his family across from them was exciting. However, the conversation did not interest her, and she ate not unhappily in silence for the most part. She politely answered the questions put to her. When she finished eating, she leaned against her mother, who put her arm around her. The feasting would continue all afternoon, but after a while her mother suggested she go and find Sariah and play. Her father agreed, and he embraced her before she left.

Ariana spent the afternoon playing in the fields with Sariah and her friends. Many games and sports had been organized in different places. Ariana would take a break back in the tent for some water and sit with different people.

Cali spent the afternoon down at the bridge. The noise of the celebration brought back too many memories of the queen's city, even though the situation was completely different. She helped bring food down to the guards who remained on duty. She was able to walk all the way across the bridge to the other side with the food. The guard who liked her was stationed there today. She brought him and his companion food, and they ate outside the first guard post. From here, the road ran due north up into the mountains where, many leagues away, one could make the crossing to the east. Cali realized that today was the first time she had been across the river since she arrived. She looked back across the river at her new home, and the beauty of it gave her a sense of peace.

When the evening came and the sun was almost setting, Ariana and Sariah went home to change. Caleb and most of the other young men had stopped to eat more before changing, as the afternoon of sports had made them hungry. Their appetite was nothing unusual. One of the young men made a joke at how long the ladies took to get ready, but Hershel pointed out that they were worth the wait. Every head nodded in agreement. Even the king of Kadesh nodded in agreement. The young men ate and laughed for a bit until the king bid them to go prepare and to be on time.

As the last rays of sunshine shone above, everyone gathered in silence. Three of the elders were present, and the one named Yuria led the prayer service. He sang a song of praise to the Lord Most High in the ancient language of the people. Every time Ariana heard it, something stirred deep inside, an awe and respect for the Lord Most High. She looked up as the sunlight faded and saw the first star coming out. It was the brightest star in the sky, the center of the "hand of God." She became distracted and thought about the pendant she had received. She imagined wearing it and thought that this celebration would definitely be one of the times she would be allowed to display it. The elders were leading a responsive prayer, and Ariana closed her eyes and listened as everyone responded. For some reason, she did not. She saw in her mind a great crowd of people around her. But she was somewhere else, and the people surrounding her were not praising the Lord Most High. A battle raged in front of them, and she was filled with fear. A woman was next to her with arm around her shoulder. She was holding someone's hand to her right, and when she opened her eyes to see who it was the vision was gone. Ariana's mother behind her had noticed that she was not participating. She moved forward and put her arm around her daughter. The feeling of the arm around Ariana was not the same as in the vision she had just seen, but it comforted her. She spoke the responses as the vision completely faded. The service ended with a great shout of praise to the Lord Most High. The music started, and so did the dancing. Food and drink was also available for anyone who wanted more.

The night passed quickly, and soon came the second to the last dance, called the "dance of young love," in which almost everyone would participate. When Ariana was younger, she had danced it with Caleb, Sariah, or another cousin. Parents would take the youngest children in their arms for the dance. Sometimes the grandparents would hold a small child during the dance. For Caleb and soon Ariana as they approached the courting age, the dance was more significant. This year, Caleb was going to dance with a girl named Bethsaida, or Beth for short, whom he had met that summer while Ariana was away. He had spent the whole day with her. Ariana felt a little jealous, for she missed her brother. Sariah was asked by a boy from her town some time ago, and she had agreed, not reluctantly. Ariana would dance this night with her cousin Elim. He was kind, strong, and liked by many. When Ariana came to say hello, Elim was talking with his mother about the dance, for he had not asked anyone. He was not as worried at finding someone or at the significance of the dance; so he was glad to agree to dance with Ariana. Of course, a few other girls' hearts were broken when they learned of this pairing. But the girls could always hope for next year, and they had learned that waiting until the last day was not always wise. The musicians announced the dance, and the dancers found their respective partners. Ariana was pleased with her choice when Elim had found her and escorted her to the dance area. The music started slowly and sweetly. The couples swirled around the dance floor, and Ariana smiled as she passed Sariah. Ariana saw many relatives, but what caught her eye the most was the sight of Caleb and Beth. The look of love was strong in their eyes. She was also surprised and delighted to see Cali dancing with the guard that liked her. At the same time, Ariana made sure not to ignore Elim and to be the perfect dance partner. The dance seemed to last a long time, but as the familiar ending to the music approached, Ariana wished that she could remain in the moment. The dance ended, and the people clapped. Many, like Caleb, stole a kiss from their partners at the end of the dance. Then the music began again, and the last dance started. It was called the "dance of the harvest," and every family would come together to form a circle. The men would go one way around the circle, and the women the other way. The movement was a little complicated, but everyone learned the steps. You would pass by other dancers and then stop and dance with the person opposite you at that point. Then everyone would join hands in the circle and go to the left or to the right, depending on the music. The dance was a lot of fun, and the families would be laughing together when it ended. After this dance, the families would remain together in the circle. Everyone would join hands together and sing a song of praise and thanks to the Lord Most High. Then the spiritual leader, in this case the Elder Yuria, ended the evening in prayer. When the prayer was finished, everyone headed home or to lodgings. Cali walked ahead of Hershel and Miriam with Ariana and Sariah on each arm. The sweet fragrance of flowers filled the air, and the stars shone bright overhead. Ariana was so happy and filled with joy that she believed that this day was the best of her life.

Many tears were shed in the following days as people were leaving to go home. Hershel had given the pendant that Cali made for Ariana to her father, his brother, and explained the word that had come to them concerning it. Caleb and Ariana were the last two to leave for their home, traveling with their older brother Saul and his family. Caleb would have preferred to go back with Beth, but her family had no room. Plus, he also missed his sister. Ariana and her family said goodbye to Sariah's family early in the morning. Sariah, Ariana, Miriam, and Cali all cried, and even Caleb and Hershel shed a tear or two. Then, the travelers were on the road headed for home. Ariana remembered how Cali bent down, and they embraced each other. Ariana kissed her cheek and could still taste the salt from her tears and smell the sweet smell of her hair. She remembered her new friend every night of the journey home, and tears of joy and sorrow were in her eyes as she lay down to sleep.

A week later, Ariana's family arrived home. Caleb was glad to be back, but Ariana was still sad. Her mother sensed this gloom as they spent time together in the following days. Ariana told her mother all the things that had happened that summer except for the night of the storm with Cali. Caleb engaged his sister in a friendly sword fight with wooden training swords. He easily beat her the first time; so the next time he let her win without her knowing. Their cousin had given Caleb a set of throwing knives in which he was not really interested; so he gave them to Ariana. She spent some time practicing with them, and she turned out to be a good thrower. But soon she put them away and would not use them for some time. Things gradually returned to normal.

Several weeks passed, and one night Ariana was awakened just after getting to sleep by the sound of horses outside her house. The sound of horsemen was nothing new to her, but the hour was a little late for riders. Ariana was still half asleep when she heard the sound of voices coming from downstairs. Then she heard the sound of raised voices again, particularly her mother's. She could not decipher what the speakers were saying, for their voices were lowered. She heard her older sister and brother talking, then silence. Now that she was wide awake, she tried to listen for any conversation. She heard someone going outside, probably the riders, tending to their horses and seeking lodging for the night. Ariana got up and stood by her door, but she heard nothing. She felt like she was waiting forever for any sound. She was just about to give up when she heard footsteps coming up the stairs. She could hear her mother and father talking as they came up. Her heart was filled with fear, and her mind was racing with thoughts. What was the news? Were they coming to her room? All she could think of was that something had happened to Sariah. Her mother and father came into the room and found her awake and sitting on the bed. She saw her mother's eyes moist with tears and instantly panicked.

"What has happened?" she cried. "Is Sariah all right?"

"Sariah is fine," said her father, "but something has happened that you should know."

Ariana's parents sat on each side of her, and her mother put her arms around her shoulders.

Her father continued, "The woman that you met named Cali is gone."

Ariana sat dumbfounded at this news. She was shocked.

"We are all grieved by this report," her father said, and he, too, put his arm around her.

As the reality of the news hit, tears rolled down Ariana's cheeks, but she was still too surprised to cry as hard as she would later. She just asked, "What happened?"

"The riders who came told us that she went down to the great bridge like she always did. But this time, she walked out into the middle of the bridge and jumped into the water. The guards on the bridge did not see her again, for the water flows swiftly out of the land. I'm afraid we must conclude that she is dead." He paused and then added, "I don't know why she would do such a thing."

But Ariana felt that she knew. The trials that Cali had suffered still haunted her, and she could not be free of them, even though the Lord surely forgave her. Ariana did not understand the depths of such pain. She spent some time with her parents and siblings that night, for they joined together in times of joy and sorrow. She said very little, though, and nobody knew what Cali had told her. The painful story filled Ariana's thoughts for the next few weeks, and somewhere deep inside she developed a subconscious hatred towards outsiders. She thought about all of the cruelty Cali had suffered at the hands of these people in other lands, and she hoped that she would never see anyone from outside Jeshuryn. They were all barbarians. She harbored this hatred in her heart, where it stayed buried for years. From that day forward, she never danced the "dance of young love." She would always think of Cali dancing it in her beautiful white dress, and the memory would make her cry.

Even now, six years later, the memory was still potent at times like tonight. While Hershel and Arden were on the waters outside of Tyre, Ariana sat outside under the stars. She found herself lost in their beauty and the majesty of the heavens. So much had changed since the night she had heard of Cali's death. Ariana thought of her uncle Hershel for a moment, wondering if he was home or away. Last she knew, he had left with his sons on another voyage across the sea. She wondered if he looked up at the stars at night and thought of home. If she knew that he was doing just that right now and praying for her, the knowledge would not have surprised her, but it would have made her smile.

Chapter 10

The Hill of the Prophets

Outside the great walled city of Tyre is a hill called the Hill of the Prophets. The crossroads intersect to the west of the hill, and the road to the city runs along the north side of the hill, giving an impressive eastern view of the city from above. Many years past, an old man had stood on the hilltop and preached to the travelers on the road. The hill became known as the Hill of the Prophet. Five years before Arden's arrest, a down-and-out prophet from the city decided to go up to the hill. At first, he went to find some inspiration in the grand view of the city. Then as he stood on the hill, the idea occurred to him that the travelers on the road might need some advice from a prophet. So he started giving advice (for money, of course) to people passing by. Soon he was making a pretty good living for himself; then other prophets from the city also decided to try their luck on the hill. Over the next three years, the business caught on.

During the summer season, many travelers used the road; so plenty of people were around. The prophets agreed to share space on the hill, which soon became a crowded place as others came from the city to sell water and food to the travelers. The Hill of the Prophets was almost a miniature town during the day. All kinds of prophets would offer to tell you the future, the past, where to go, what to avoid, etc. Some were dressed in robes, others in fancy clothes with bright colors and symbols of their gods. Some shouted loudly, while others were quiet. Soon you could find almost any sort of prophecy you wanted. As the early mornings were usually slow, some of the prophets would arrive early to take their usual spots and have a morning meal before working, if you could call what they did work. Some of them even had agreements with places in the city to steer people their way. "Such and such god advises you to stay at the inn next to the market square; tell them the prophet of the sun sent you." Business was going pretty well for most of these prophets. The field pretty much narrowed itself to twenty or so prophets. New ones would appear, but unless they were appealing and told people what they wanted to hear, they would not last.

One day in the early morning when the prophets and sellers from the city went up to the hill, they found a man there holding the lead of a white horse. His hair was short, and his clean-shaven face had a stern and commanding appearance. He wore a dark gray cloak, a blue shirt with a design on it, a leather belt with a sword, and leather boots. His clothes and boots were dusty from the road. He sat high up on the hill, away from the road. The others naturally thought he was a new prophet, just based on his appearance. But for six whole days, he sat in place and said nothing to anyone. Most of the time, he had a book in his hand which he would read and then speak to himself. Nobody saw him leave or arrive, and nobody spoke to him. Every day he would come down in the midst of the busy time and walk through the crowd as if observing everything. Most people ignored him. Few would meet his gaze, and those who did would turn away. None could stand his piercing eyes that seemed to look right into their hearts.

Finally, on the seventh day, he rose from his spot on the hill and walked down towards the road. On a ledge that was higher than the ones where any of the prophets stood, he stopped and raised his hands. The prophets below stopped speaking when they saw him, and a hush came over the crowd, not just from the sight of him. The air felt strange, like heaviness had filled it. He stared into the crowd until all of the people were silent. Then he spoke to the crowd.

"People of Tyre, hear me! Woe to you who seek your way from men instead of the Lord Most High! Listen to what the Scriptures say.

"Does not wisdom call out? Does not understanding raise her voice? On the heights along the way, where the paths meet, she takes her stand; beside the gates leading into the city, at the entrances, she cries aloud: 'To you, O men, I call out; I raise my voice to all mankind. You who are simple: gain prudence; you who are foolish: gain understanding. Listen, for I have worthy things to say; I open my lips to speak what is right. My mouth speaks what is true, for my lips detest wickedness. All the words of my mouth are just; none of them is crooked or perverse. To the discerning, all of them are right; they are faultless to those who have knowledge. Choose my instruction instead of silver, knowledge rather than choice gold, for wisdom is more precious than rubies, and nothing you desire can compare with her.

"'I, wisdom, dwell together with prudence; I possess knowledge and discretion. To fear the Lord Most High is to hate evil. I hate pride and arrogance, evil behavior and perverse speech. Counsel and sound judgment are mine; I have understanding and power. By me, kings reign, and rulers make laws that are just. By me, princes govern, and all nobles who rule on earth. I love those who love me, and those who seek me find me.

"'With me are riches and honor, enduring wealth and prosperity. My fruit is better than fine gold; what I yield surpasses choice silver. I walk in the way of righteousness, along the paths of justice, bestowing wealth on those who love me and making their treasuries full.

"'The Lord Most High brought me forth as the first of His works, before His deeds of old; I was appointed from eternity, from the beginning, before the world began. When there were no oceans, I was given birth; when there were no springs abounding with water, before the mountains were settled in place, before the hills, I was given birth, before He made the earth or its fields or any of the dust of the world. I was there when He set the heavens in place, when He marked out the horizon on the face of the deep, when He established the clouds above and fixed securely the fountains of the deep, when He gave the sea its boundary so that the waters would not overstep His command, and when He marked out the foundations of the earth. Then I was the craftsman at His side. I was filled with delight day after day, rejoicing always in His presence, rejoicing in His whole world and delighting in mankind.

"'Now then, my children, listen to me; blessed are those who keep my ways. Listen to my instruction and be wise; do not ignore it. Blessed is the man who listens to me, watching daily at my doors, waiting at my doorway. For whoever finds me finds life and receives favor from the Lord Most High. But whoever fails to find me harms himself; all who hate me love death.'" [1]

When he finished, he turned and began to walk back up the hill.

"Who are you?" shouted a woman from the crowd.

He turned back towards the crowd. "My name is Ildera," he said.

"Don't go!" shouted another, "tell us more."

"I will return in seven days," he said, and he walked back up the hill, mounted his horse, and rode away. The crowd was so captivated by his words that not many spoke. The prophets were furious, because they knew that the first line that he spoke was about them. Finally, the leader of the prophets spoke to the crowd. "Who is this man that speaks to you? Why do you listen to him? Where is this Lord Most High? Have you seen Him? Haven't those of you who put an offering in the cup of my god been blessed?" The other prophets started speaking as well, and the noise of the crowd returned as people began to move about their business again.

Seven days later, Ildera appeared again, sitting in the same spot as before, and the prophets and the sellers came up the hill. Ildera sat without moving, watching and waiting. Many people from the city who had heard him speak or heard rumors of his last appearance came out just to see what would happen. They sat in the shade waiting. The sellers enjoyed the extra business and were thinking of spreading the news of this new prophet. They would tell travelers and point to the strange man on the hill. The other prophets did not know what to expect. They were pleased with the large crowd but felt uneasiness in their hearts. Their hearts were like a thunder storm approaching. Though the approaching clouds are black, if you are looking the other way, the false deception of blue sky is all you see.

Finally when the crowd was at its peak, Ildera stood. He walked down to the same ledge where he had stood before, above the prophets.

"People of Tyre," he shouted. "Hear again the words of the Lord Most High." His voice sounded like thunder, and the people fell silent. The merchants were thrilled at this new prophecy because it promised more business; many in the crowd were waiting with excitement.

Staring down at the prophets, Ildera said: "A truthful witness does not deceive, but a false witness pours out lies. The mocker seeks wisdom and finds none, but knowledge comes easily to the discerning." Looking out to the crowd, he continued: "Stay away from a foolish man, for you will not find knowledge on his lips. The wisdom of the prudent is to give thought to their ways, but the folly of fools is deception. Fools mock at making amends for sin, but goodwill is found among the upright. Each heart knows its own bitterness, and no one else can share its joy. The house of the wicked will be destroyed, but the tent of the upright will flourish." [2]

A murmur went through the crowd at these words. A brave traveler on a horse yelled, "What would you have us do, then?"

Ildera continued without pausing. His voice was softer but equally as penetrating to the crowd. "There is a way that seems right to a man, but in the end it leads to death. Even in laughter, the heart may ache, and joy may end in grief. The faithless will be fully repaid for their ways, and the good man rewarded for his. A simple man believes anything, but a prudent man gives thought to his steps. To man belong the plans of the heart, but from the Lord comes the reply of the tongue. All a man's ways seem innocent to him, but motives are weighed by the Lord. Commit to the Lord whatever you do, and your plans will succeed." [3]

Turning back to the prophets, he said: "The Lord works out everything for His own ends, even the wicked for a day of disaster. The Lord detests all the proud of heart. Be sure of this: they will not go unpunished. Through love and faithfulness, sin is atoned for; through the fear of the Lord, a man avoids evil." Staring back at the crowd, he said: "When a man's ways are pleasing to the Lord, He makes even his enemies live at peace with him. Better a little with righteousness than much gain with injustice. In his heart a man plans his course, but the Lord determines his steps." [4]

At this pronouncement, Ildera finished and walked back up the hill. With his back to the crowd, he stood with arms raised in the air, speaking in a strange language (although nobody could hear him). The words had a strange effect on the crowd, focusing their thoughts inward. The other prophets felt a sickening sense of fear in their hearts which they could not explain. They refused to believe that this man was somehow speaking from any source other than himself, as they were. They took a few minutes to recover, but then they began to speak again to the crowd. The calm that had descended over the crowd slowly dissipated, and the prior noise level returned. However, several of the potential customers of the prophets did not stay after hearing the words of Ildera. This loss of business really irritated the prophets.

One old woman had come from the city with her grandchildren to hear Ildera speak. When she heard that a prophet had used the name of the Lord Most High, she was filled with amazement. She had brought with her a loaf of bread, baked in the traditional way. Her youngest granddaughter was ill, and she and the other grandchildren had carried her along. The woman was too old to climb the hill to reach Ildera; so she sent the kids up with instructions. They went up by a path that led around the hill from behind and finally reached him. He was sitting on a mat on the ground under a large tree, reading an old book and speaking strange words. The children were frightened and would not come closer. He stopped reading and motioned them over.

"Sir," the eldest child said, "our grandmother has sent us with bread for you to eat and water for you to drink."

Ildera stopped reading and turned towards them. Inside, he was filled with compassion at the sight before him. An older boy was carrying a young girl in his arms, and another smaller boy had the bread and water. The boys were tired and scared.

"Do not be afraid!" he said, "come closer and sit."

The boys approached, and the younger placed the bread and water at his feet.

"What else did your grandmother say?" he asked kindly.

"Our sister is sick," they said, "she said you could make her well. We will do whatever you say."

"Do not be troubled," he replied. He stood up and took the girl in his arms. She was pale and feverish. "I cannot make her well," he said. Tears filled the younger boy's eyes at these words. "However," Ildera continued with a gleam in his eye, "the Spirit of the Lord Most High can. Do you believe so?"

"Yes," said the older boy.

"What about you?" Ildera asked the younger.

"Yes," he answered through the tears.

"Then you must help me by believing. Ask the Lord Most High in your heart to heal your sister as I ask out loud." He placed the girl on the mat and sat behind her. He then motioned for the boys to sit down next to him and told them to close their eyes. Then he said, "Lord, I thank You that You care for this child and desire her to be healed. We ask that You heal her right now from any sickness or disease that is in her body." Ildera put his hand on her forehead as he prayed. The girl stirred from her sleep and opened her eyes. The boys heard her and opened their eyes to see her wide awake. They cried out with joy at this sight. She sat up and her brothers embraced her. Ildera took the bread, thanked the Lord Most High for it, and gave her a piece to eat and some water to drink. She drank thirstily, and her pallor disappeared. Ildera shared the bread and water with the boys as well. Once the girl was able to stand, Ildera sent the children back to their grandmother.

"Tell your grandmother this: the city of Tyre is no place to raise children. Settle your affairs and return here in two weeks. I will be waiting for you." The children left with smiles on their faces and joy in their hearts.

At the end of the day, most of the prophets waited on the hill until the crowds had left. Then they went up the hill to confront Ildera. When they arrived, he was speaking to himself in a language that none of them could understand. "What is it that you want?" asked their leader. "Is it money? Are you trying to take our business? We have all agreed to pay you one hundred gold coins if you leave. We will never admit this offer to the people; so don't even think of telling them." The leader took the bag of coins from one of the men and held it out.

Ildera stopped speaking to himself and laughed slightly. "You have heard my voice, but not my words," he said. His tone was not haughty but gentle, with a hint of sadness. "I say only what I am led to say, and I must stay here until my Lord tells me otherwise. Even if you offered ten thousand gold coins, I could not take them."

"We have no wish for violence," said another, "but consider the threat that you are to our business. You must understand our position." He tried to sound tough, but the longer the prophets stood there, the greater was the fear in their hearts.

"We will give you seven days to answer," said the leader, and they walked away.

On the seventh day, Ildera returned again. Instead of going to the leaders, he stood again on the hill in front of all of the people. A cry went up as people noticed him. Soon a great crowd had gathered. Ildera raised his hands in the air, and the crowd quieted. The prophets said nothing, but they were filled with fear and anxiety about what he might say.

Ildera began by speaking loudly. "Wisdom calls aloud in the street; she raises her voice in the public squares. At the head of the noisy streets, she cries out; in the gateways of the city, she makes her speech. 'How long will you simple ones love your simple ways? How long will mockers delight in mockery and fools hate knowledge? If you had responded to my rebuke, I would have poured out my heart to you and made my thoughts known to you. But since you rejected me when I called and no one gave heed when I stretched out my hand, since you ignored all my advice and would not accept my rebuke, I in turn will laugh at your disaster. I will mock when calamity overtakes you, when calamity overtakes you like a storm, when disaster sweeps over you like a whirlwind, when distress and trouble overwhelm you.

"'Then they will call to me, but I will not answer. They will look for me but will not find me. Since they hated knowledge and did not choose to fear the Lord Most High, since they would not accept my advice and spurned my rebuke, they will eat the fruit of their ways and be filled with the fruit of their schemes. The waywardness of the simple will kill them, and the complacency of fools will destroy them. But whoever listens to me will live in safety and be at ease, without fear of harm." [5]

Murmuring again arose in the crowd. The prophets sneered but said nothing. The words had a chilling effect on the crowd, and many felt conviction in their hearts for their greed and foolish plotting.

Ildera continued. "The lips of a king speak as an oracle, and his mouth should not betray justice. Honest scales and balances are from the Lord Most High; all the weights in the bag are of His making. Kings detest wrongdoing, for a throne is established through righteousness. Kings take pleasure in honest lips; they value a man who speaks the truth. A king's wrath is a messenger of death, but a wise man will appease it. When a king's face brightens, it means life; his favor is like a rain cloud in spring. How much better to get wisdom than gold, to choose understanding rather than silver! The highway of the upright avoids evil; he who guards his way guards his life." [6]

"Ha!" one of the prophets sneered. "We don't have a king; we follow a queen."

"I know the woman of whom you speak; she is loud, undisciplined, and without knowledge. She sits at the door of her house, on a seat at the highest point of the city, calling out to those who pass by, who go straight on their way. 'Let all who are simple come in here!' she says to those who lack judgment. 'Stolen water is sweet; food eaten in secret is delicious!' But little do they know that the dead are there, that her guests are in the depths of the grave." [7]

Then he turned and went back up the hill. A seeming sadness stole into his voice at the mention of the queen, but few perceived it. Although no great love for her existed among the people present, they knew better than to speak against her in public and were surprised that anyone would be so bold.

The prophets were outraged, but too afraid to say anything. Now, even the other prophets who were quiet could stand no more and decided to have him killed. Because they were too afraid to do the deed themselves, they all contributed money to hire someone to do it. They found the perfect man for the job: Morgoth, an ex-soldier turned torturer/executioner for the city. He wore all black clothing and a mask like a skull to scare his victims. He was so nasty that he actually did deter crime in the city, where money was more valuable than life! Morgoth planned to ride his horse up to the hill during the peak hour and slay this prophet of the true God. A week later, the day came, and the prophets were filled with secret excitement, knowing what would happen.

Despite Ildera's previous words, even a larger crowd came that week to see this mysterious prophet of the Lord Most High. The merchants, who were thrilled, planned to ask him to move to another spot away from these prophets under the pretense of giving him a center stage for himself. But they really wanted to sell their goods at both places, for they knew that the other prophets who were not happy with him would take action sooner or later. They did not know that the plan was set for that day, or they would have bribed the other prophets to abandon their plan.

Once again, Ildera took his place on the hill and spoke. "Listen, my children, to your father's instruction, and do not forsake your mother's teaching. They will be a garland to grace your head and a chain to adorn your neck. My children, if sinners entice you, do not give in to them. If they say, 'Come along with us; let's lie in wait for someone's blood. Let's waylay some harmless soul; let's swallow them alive, like the grave, and whole, like those who go down to the pit. We will get all sorts of valuable things and fill our houses with plunder. Throw in your lot with us, and we will share a common purse,' do not go along with them. Do not set foot on their paths, for their feet rush into sin. They are swift to shed blood.

"How useless it is to spread a net in full view of all the birds! These men lie in wait for their own blood; they waylay only themselves! Such is the end of all who go after ill-gotten gain; it takes away the lives of those who get it." [8]

The silent crowd watched intently as Ildera walked up to the next ledge above where he normally stood. Looking down at the head prophet, he said, "As surely as I stand here today, blood will be spilled on this hill today. Then the people will know the truth."

When he finished speaking, voices whispered from the edge of the crowd, and the people turned and saw a rider approaching on a black horse. He was dressed in all black with a skull mask. Gasps rose from the crowd as they realized that this rider was the evil Morgoth. He rode with all fury up from the city towards the hill. A few in the crowd turned towards Ildera, who stood without moving. A few of the prophets thought he would surely run away. But he just stood there, not even drawing his sword. As Morgoth came closer, the crowd moved back to the other side of the road, away from the prophets. Some of them even left their positions and went to the other side of the road.

Finally Morgoth reached the crowd and rode towards the head prophet's altar. Morgoth's horse jumped over the altar and raced up the hill towards Ildera. As the horse was jumping, Morgoth drew his sword, a long, curved blade. Ildera did not move. Suddenly the horse was seized with madness and reared up, causing Morgoth to drop his sword in the rocks. The handle fell into a crevice, and the blade stuck up out of the ground. Morgoth's immediate reaction was to draw his knife, which would work just as well. Furious, Morgoth kicked his horse to urge it forward. However, the horse would not go forward but sidestepped to the left. Once again, he kicked the horse with all his might. The brutal kick caused the horse to turn sideways and fall to the ground, throwing Morgoth off and across the rocks onto his own sword, killing him. At the same time, many in the crowd saw two giant men in white on both sides of Ildera. The crowd, filled with fear, ran away towards the city accompanied by several of the prophets. Even the merchants left their stalls behind and ran. The remaining prophets were also terrified, but they did not want to run before the people. They were speechless and could not comprehend what had just happened. They saw the men in white, shining as bright as the sun. The closer the prophets looked, the more fear filled them. They could see white armor and flaming swords in the hands of Ildera's protectors. Their faces were too terrible to gaze upon. And in the middle stood Ildera: confident, unwavering. The crowd was going down the hill back to the city when the prophets turned and ran. Just then, the black horse got up from the ground. Ildera moved to stop it, but it ran away as fast as it could. It ran right through the prophets and trampled some of them, including the leader.

Ildera stood alone on the hill. He gave thanks to the Lord Most High for saving him from defeat. Yet despite the victory, Ildera was sad at the deaths, even for the leader of the prophets. Ildera, who also loved horses, wanted to stop the black horse and heal it from its many years of cruel treatment. He left the hill victorious but with great sadness in his heart.

Chapter 11

The City of Tyre

In the early evening, the ship carrying Arden to the strange lands approached the city of Tyre. Arden could see that the city was much larger than Old Harbor. Buildings lined the dockside, and the streets were busy with people. Many other ships at least as big as their own were berthed here. Even more pronounced was the city behind the docks. The city was large and impressive looking. Massive stone walls guarded the city, and behind them were many rooftops with several towers of stone rising in the midst of them. Behind the city to the left, Arden saw a hill that was almost a small mountain from his perspective. The sun sank low in the sky behind this hill, and its shadow cast the center of the city into darkness. As the ship approached the dock, the noise of the port increased. The smell of rotten fish blew by for a minute, and Arden felt like he was going to vomit. Then the wind shifted, and the smell of food cooking filled the air. It smelled delicious, and Arden's stomach went from nauseated to hungry so quickly that he felt sick. The ship made for a specific dock and reached it quickly. The crew cast lines to secure the ship. Arden stayed out of the way the best he could. Hershel had bid him to stay well back in the ship so as not to be noticed from shore, and Arden reluctantly agreed. He had already found so much to see here, and he longed to be right at the bow watching everything. An official from the port came aboard and conducted the formalities quickly, as he had boarded this ship so many times before. Hershel and his older son Jorham were going to go ashore and take care of some of their business before the sun set; so Hershel's other son, Bezalel, took Arden below to eat dinner. Arden was disappointed, but at the same time he was tired and longed to get some sleep. Bezalel advised him to retire early, as he would have a long day tomorrow. So he went to bed and was soon fast asleep. Before he had left, Hershel had asked the captain to keep the other two prisoners on board, but the captain said that he had no right to do so. The captain urged the two men to spend the night on board, but when they refused, the Captain then read from a legal document, releasing them from his charge and confirming their exile. He gave both men money to start them off in their new life, advising them to seek lodging and be conservative with the money. Lavin was surprised at the gift but said nothing. Marcus was ungrateful because he wanted more money. Both reclaimed the possessions that they were allowed to bring on board with them, and then some of the crew escorted them off the ship.

The exiles did heed the captain's advice somewhat by securing lodging at a portside inn. Then they went to the tavern to get food and drink. First, they had a drink to cheer them up, and then they toasted their freedom. Of course, several people overheard them, including the bartender. He gave them a free round and inquired of their situation. When they said that they were from Caladen, he was secretly overjoyed that he had made a good choice. He gave them another round free, and they ordered food. The bartender excused himself for a moment and stepped into the back. The food took some time to arrive, but the exiles really did not notice the delay. Just after they had finished the meal and several more drinks, two attractive ladies entered the tavern. They immediately approached Lavin and Marcus and welcomed them in the name of the queen. They extended an invitation to the queen's palace tonight. Forgetting that they had already paid for a room where they were, the men were enticed to leave right away with the ladies. A carriage outside was waiting to take them to the city of the queen.

When Hershel returned with his son, he was upset that the men were released, but he understood the captain's position. The captain had sent a contact from the port to spy on the prisoners. Hours later, the spy came aboard and told the captain what had happened. The captain woke Hershel up and told him as Hershel had asked him to do if he heard any news. Hershel tore his shirt in anger.

"Even a three-year-old child has more self-control than those two!" he said. The captain smiled, and they both laughed.

"What will you do now?" the captain asked.

"We will leave right away and stay in the city tonight with some distant relatives and friends," he replied. "Tomorrow, we will start the journey home."

"I will take care of unloading your cargo and making sure that it gets delivered to the proper places," said the captain.

"Thank you," said Hershel. "I will send my cousin Eli to help you. You have seen him before."

"Of course," said the captain, "he has helped us before when we needed him."

In a very short time, Hershel and his younger son Bezalel were on deck. "May the Lord Most High bless you and keep you," said Hershel to the captain.

"And may His Spirit guide you safely to your home," said the captain. The men hugged quickly, and then departed.

Jorham woke Arden and helped him quickly gather all his possessions. He gave him a dark cloak to wear and instructed him to put up the hood. The captain had a horse waiting for the men on the dock, and he met them just before they emerged on deck. "Arden," he said quickly, "I am bound by law to release you from my custody, and I do so now. It is also law that I give you provisions for your journey, and I have done so by giving the money due to you to Hershel. The king of Caladen has asked me to commit you to his care. Hershel will guide you safely to Jeshuryn with the help and guidance of the Lord Most High. I bid you farewell and safe journey." With that, the captain embraced Arden briefly, and then the two walked out together. As they were leaving, the captain stooped to whisper something in Arden's ear.

Arden mounted the horse behind Jorham, who took the reins. They left the port and rode up through the city gates. Despite the midnight hour, the streets still had quite a bit of traffic on them, and the guards at the gates ignored the riders. Plus, the night air was cold; so the cloak drew no suspicion. Lamps with candles in them hung in the main streets and lit the way for them as well as the lights still coming from many homes. Arden could not tell where they were going or even how Jorham was able to navigate the streets. They turned down one side street and then rode down several more. They finally turned down another street that was a dead end and rode into a yard at the end of it. Lights were on in this house, and they dismounted and went inside. An entire family inside were sitting around a large table, awake and ready to meet them. An old woman kissed Jorham and bid both newcomers welcome. She spoke in a language that Arden could not understand, but she motioned to him and smiled. Three younger children and an older man were there as well. The children looked at Arden with friendly curiosity. A young man took Arden by the arm and led him upstairs to a bedroom. Arden lay on the bed and was soon asleep. He was not sure whose room he took or if it was an extra one, but he felt that it belonged to the young man who had led him. Arden dreamed about the sea and the large, dark city surrounding him.

By this time, the carriage carrying Lavin and Marcus was well on its way to the queen's city. The ladies had easily extracted much information from their two guests. They fed their egos with feigned affection while trying to hide any disdain they might have felt towards these drunken strangers. The men talked freely but were getting tired from the food and drink, along with the lateness of the day. The ladies gave them a smaller drink, which put them to sleep. The men would sleep for the rest of the journey, an hour or so, while dreaming their fantasies. The ladies speculated briefly on what would happen to these two men. They laughed at how arrogant the younger one was. As he was strong and full of lust, they agreed that the queen would surely kill him and drink his blood, for they knew that the queen believed that drinking blood, especially blood of the Caladenians and some others, would keep her alive forever. Many rumors circulated about this practice, but not many people really believed it was true, despite the fact that the queen never seemed to get older and nobody could tell how old she really was. One of the ladies wondered to herself if the blood would keep her young like the queen, and she wondered what the blood would do to her if she took just a little. But surely the queen would notice even a needle prick on one of the fingers, and such an experiment wasn't worth the queen's wrath. Besides, the queen might let the older one live. He was intelligent for sure, and he did not ramble on like the younger one. The queen did not tolerate fools. But he gave such valuable information so freely. *If he remains alive, though, I might have a chance to try some of his blood later,* she thought. She also wondered about the other woman with her, who once lived with one of these foreigners before he met an untimely end at the hands of the queen. Had she tried anything like stealing blood? Surely she had not. The queen would never suffer a rival. This woman was older and not someone with whom to discuss personal speculations. *In fact,* she thought, *I cannot wait until we've delivered our cargo and made our report to the queen. Then I will go my way, and Brea will go hers.*

Chapter 12

The Crossroads

Hershel's party left Tyre for the crossroads early in the morning. Arden had slept soundly the rest of the night and woke just after dawn. He ate breakfast with the family of the house, and being in a room with them felt good. Jorham arrived midway through breakfast and joined the family, as he had a little time before he and Arden would have to leave. Soon, the time came to leave, and the travelers rode the horse through the city until they met with the wagon carrying their goods on which Hershel rode. Soon Arden sat next to Hershel in front, wearing the hooded cloak that hid his face. As the day was cloudy and seemed like rain, he was still not out of place wearing the cloak. Hershel had wanted to leave earlier, but now was a better time with more people on the road to and from the city. If anyone was watching from the city wall, Hershel's group would appear no different than any other merchants on the road. Yet Hershel was apprehensive and anxious inside. He did not want to fill Arden with unnecessary panic; so he said nothing. He knew, though, that soon, if not already, the other two men from Caladen would be brought to the queen. When the queen learned that a teen boy from Caladen was traveling in her land, she would certainly send troops to bring him to her. The queen would surely guess his destination and conclude that he would be guided by someone familiar with the land. Riders from the city would easily overtake a group of traveling merchants. Hershel could not hide Arden in the back of the wagon and hope to fool any pursuers. Despite his anxiety, Hershel took several deep breaths and thought of his prayer time that morning. He was sure that the Spirit of the Lord had told him to go to the crossroads, and the answer would be there. His mind was full of questions, though. Would he have to send Arden and one of his sons ahead in hopes of outrunning any pursuers? Doing so seemed unlikely, because the travelers still needed to pass the road to Ashkelon. He forced his mind to stop asking these foolish questions. *Just trust in the Lord,* he told himself. The party came to the Hill of the Prophets, and the morning was still early enough to get through without delay. The crowd would be at its peak several hours from now.

Hershel and his companions continued for at least another two hours until they reached the crossroads. Although rain did not fall, the sky was gray, and the sun did not emerge from behind the clouds. The crossroads were on an elevated spot where you could see each of the four roads that intersected here for some distance. A stone bridge made long ago passed over the north-south road. Scattered around the crossing were remnants of stone buildings from ages past. The terrain here was fields of long grass. Near the walls, where the grass was short and green, people usually stopped to rest. An old well pump here provided drinking water and a spot to water the horses. Hershel's group stopped here, and one of the sons took the horses to get water. The other travelers here all kept to themselves today. Perhaps the gray weather did not inspire anyone to greet his fellow travelers cheerfully. Hershel took Arden up to the bridge to survey the area. The western road ahead of them was deserted, but plenty of people were traveling the north-south road. The south road would continue down the coast, and Hershel had not traveled on it. To the northwest, Arden could see mountains in the distance. The north road would take the travelers around those mountains to the east and eventually to another road that would lead to the great bridge at the top of Jeshuryn. Dark clouds lowered on the western horizon, and Hershel was sure that they would bring rain when they arrived. Arden continued to survey the northwest while Hershel waited. Hershel looked out at the north road but did not see anything that offered an answer. The south road was exactly the same. His sons had brought the horses back to the wagon, and they were ready to go. But Hershel would not leave just yet. He told them to wait a few minutes. While he was speaking, he saw a small group approaching along the east road from Tyre. A man rode on a large white horse, and he looked like he had a child with him. Next to him was an old woman on a smaller horse with several bags on the back and a child in front of her. As they came closer, Hershel could see that the man on the white horse had two children with him. Hershel felt his heart rejoicing in the presence of the Lord. Then he felt like blinders fell off, and he recognized the man who was now right in front of them. Arden, observing the rider approaching, said nothing, although he felt something unfamiliar inside.

"Blessed is the man who does not walk in the counsel of the wicked," the rider said and dismounted. [9]

"He is like a tree that flourishes, planted by the waters," [10] Hershel responded, and then he happily walked forward to embrace his friend. "Ildera, I am overjoyed at seeing you!"

"I am pleased to see you as well, old friend. I just wish we had met under better circumstances and had more time," Ildera replied. He took the children off of his horse and the old woman's. "Can I ask your sons to attend to these people while we talk?" he said. Immediately, Hershel's sons came and took the old woman and the children to their wagon for water and food. One son took both horses to get water. Ildera gestured for Hershel to follow him across the bridge to the western road. When Arden did not move, Ildera said, "You, too, young man; join us. For this talk concerns you as well. By the way, my name is Ildera, and I am pleased to meet you." He shook Arden's hand, and the three made their way to a small section of stone wall out of earshot of everyone else at the crossroads.

"I bring you ill tidings," Ildera began. "The queen is aware of this young man - sorry, Arden - and that he is traveling north with merchants to Jeshuryn. Riders have left Tyre, and a small force will be here in less than an hour." Arden gasped at this news out of surprise and shock that this man could know so much. Ildera put his hand on Arden's shoulder, and the friendly weight reminded Arden of the king for some reason. "Nevertheless, we have no reason to give up hope. I have been in deep thought and prayer about this danger, and I have a proposal for the both of you. But you must decide quickly. Hershel, I am prepared to make an exchange with you. I will take Arden with me and lead him to Jeshuryn if you will take this woman and her children to the north with you. They have relatives in Nescor that will shelter them. The woman is a believer in the Lord Most High, and the city of Tyre will not be safe for her and her grandchildren. Here is the plan: have your sons ride ahead on the north road. You will catch up to them at the end of the day. Any of the queen's forces will not think to question solitary riders. As for you, proceed along on your wagon; it should have enough room for all of you. If the queen's soldiers should ask, you are taking your mother and children to Nescor. These children are too young to be the one for whom they are searching, and they are obviously native to this land. Arden will ride with me."

Hershel stood in deep thought. "Won't they stop us?" said Arden.

"We will be taking a different path," said Ildera.

"Aahh," said Hershel. "Now it is clear to me why I was led to wait here."

"I don't understand," said Arden.

"I'm sorry," said Ildera. "I know that I have suddenly thrust a lot of changes on you. I am familiar with a lesser-known way to get to Jeshuryn. We will take the western road. Likely, someone will see us go that way, and the bulk of the forces will come after us. But we have several advantages. Their horses will be tired, and they will have to rest here while trying to get information. They will still send riders to the north and south to cover all of the roads. My horse will outrun them easily, and they will not go farther than the old city, which we will reach before dark. But more importantly, you will need to trust me. Hershel will need to assure you that I am trustworthy."

"Arden," Hershel said, "I trust this man with my life. For many years, he has helped the people of Jeshuryn, and he is always welcome in our land should he choose to go there. He is a servant of the King of Kings who has traveled throughout all of these lands. I know of no one else who could bring you safely to Jeshuryn via the western road."

"It seems I have no choice," said Arden.

"Oh, but you do have a choice," said Ildera. "We can present the way that we feel is best, but you must make the choice. I would not force anyone to do anything that he didn't want to do. You have several alternatives. First, we could ride north and outrun these pursuers. But other spies on the road might see us, and we will be closer to the queen's city than here. If they ride out in force, we may not be able to escape. Second, we could ride south, but that road would take us the wrong way. The only way to reach Jeshuryn would be to take a ship north to Nescor. That way is possible, but the chances of success are not so good. The western road is long but not dangerous, as long as you are with me. To reach the southern edge of Jeshuryn, you must cross a desert.

That journey will be a challenge, but not impossible either. So Arden, the choice is yours. Please ask any questions you have, but time is of the essence."

"How did you know how to find us?" he asked.

"I was led by the Spirit of the Lord to the outskirts of Tyre to speak to the people and to wait for something. That something was you. I was always planning to take the western road when leaving. Although this way is longer for me because my home is north of Jeshuryn, my heart desires to go this way, for I have friends along this path that I would like to see. The woman with me brought news of your arrival and the impending pursuit, for she was privy to the talk of the city guards. It would be an honor for me if you came with me, and I think that this way is the right path for you."

"I see," said Arden, because he could not think of anything more important sounding to say. Turning to Hershel, he said, "What do you think I should do?"

"I would go with Ildera," he replied. "And when you get to Jeshuryn, we will meet there and speak of our journey."

"Then I choose to go the western road with Ildera," said Arden.

"Then let us begin at once," said Ildera.

The three men walked back to the wagon, and Hershel called everyone else together and explained the plan. The children looked sad when they heard that Ildera was leaving them, but he took the children in his arms and blessed them. Then he embraced the old woman. She bowed before him and then took the children to the wagon. Hershel's sons took Arden's pack and loaded it on Ildera's horse. They embraced Arden and bid him farewell. They showed no fear for him, and this confidence reassured him. Then Hershel embraced Arden and blessed him in the name of the Lord Most High. Arden felt a tear in his eye, and he was sad to part from this wise and kind man. Hershel's sons left and rode their horses north. Ildera and Hershel embraced and said farewell. They both started back to their charges, and then Ildera stopped and turned.

"Wait," he said. "There is something I need to tell you." He went to Hershel and whispered something in his ear. Arden saw Hershel's eyes brighten at whatever was Ildera had said.

"Truly?" Hershel asked. "It's a miracle. How?"

"It is a story for another day, my friend. But I thought you should know," said Ildera, and he smiled as he turned and came to Arden. "All right, Arden. My horse, Liberty, is one of the best horses in the land." Liberty neighed when his name was mentioned. "We need to ride with all swiftness now." Arden mounted the horse and sat behind Ildera. The wagon with Hershel and his new family were now on the north road. Ildera turned Liberty so that he could look back at the east road. At the farthest edge of their sight, they could barely make out a group of men riding black horses. Ildera knew that these riders were the men from the city, and Arden guessed so as well. Ildera turned and set out on the west road. Ildera kept Liberty at a walk until he was out of earshot from the crossroad, and then Liberty leapt forward with all speed. Arden was amazed that this horse could run so fast and continue for so long. Liberty galloped at full speed until the riders were well out of sight from the crossroads and then some. Then Ildera stopped near a pool of water at the roadside, and he and Arden dismounted so that Liberty could get some water.

"We are making for the city of Lon, which is between Tyre and a region once known as Karchemish. The city is in ruins and deserted. If any riders follow us, they will not enter the city. They will go no farther, because they believe it is haunted, along with the rest of the land after it. Of course, it's not," he laughed, seeing the look of concern on Arden's face. "But it is still some ways away, and we need to get there before nightfall."

"Do you think that they are following us?" Arden asked.

"I'm quite sure that they are," said Ildera. "I would imagine that someone at the crossroads saw us and told them. The good news is that everyone else is safe. But as the riders themselves didn't actually see us, they will always question whether or not we really came this way because it seems foolish to them."

So the two men mounted Liberty again and rode at a fair pace down the road. The road had been dirt, but now Arden could see paving stones here and there on the road. The fields were gone, and the road seemed to be on a ridge with marshes on the right and small lakes on the left. The road curved to the left for some ways and then to the right for quite some time until it reached a forest. Ildera and Arden passed what was probably an old gate, and the road was no longer dirt but all stone pavers. Liberty's soft clopping in the dirt was now quite loud as the metal shoes landed on the stone. But the road was flat and still in good condition. Arden looked ahead and saw that the road seemed to go straight on forever in one continuous direction.

The travelers continued until Arden had lost all track of time, but he felt it had to be mid afternoon at the earliest. He had felt hunger in his stomach since the first gate, where he judged it must have been noon. He and Ildera seemed to be making good time, though, as far as he could tell. He could not see anyone behind them, and no one else was on the road. They slowed as they came to another large, stone gate. As they passed the gate, the road began to change. The paving stones were no longer consistent, and patches of dirt between them in stretches where grass grew became more and more frequent. Soon, Arden could see no trace of the stone road. For some reason, Arden found this lack of a civilized road slightly disheartening. Yet the grassy path appeared to continue straight before them, as far as he could see. Then, a very slight rain began to fall. Arden and Ildera stopped and dismounted, taking refuge under a large tree. Arden took rain gear from his pack and changed into a light jacket, pants, and his favorite hat, all waterproof. Ildera did not change except to put on a hat with a short brim and a chin strap to keep it on tightly. Arden almost laughed when he thought about how different they looked. Anyone meeting them on the road would surely be puzzled by these strange companions. Several large stone structures loomed ahead, and they walked down to them rather than riding. Ildera decided that they needed a short rest. They went into a stone shelter by the side of the road, which was cool inside, but not unpleasant. Arden could see the remnants of the stone road again as he passed under the archway. Ildera took some food and water from a pack on Liberty and shared it with Arden. He blessed it first, and because Arden was so used to blessings at home, he didn't even notice.

Ildera sat down on what was perhaps a bench at one time and took off his hat. Arden sat across from him and for the first time saw a glimpse of age in the face of his companion. Maybe he was much older than he appeared. Ildera spoke to Arden, and once again his words were calming and reassuring. The rain picked up and fell steadily as they sat there.

"I know that you are probably questioning your decision to come this way. I promise you that you made the right choice."

"What is this place?"

"Various ruins stand along this road. Some are guard posts, some resting places for travelers. This road is very old. In fact, it is the oldest road in the land. It once ran between the sea and the great kingdom of Midercia. Once this settlement was a great and happy place," said Ildera sadly. "The road was full of travelers: merchants, minstrels, messengers on business for the King, or people traveling to meet relatives or loved ones far away. I would think travelers and tradesman journeyed far from here, even to your country."

Of course, Arden thought, *I've heard many stories of travels long ago to distant lands.* And the stories of the first king suddenly became more real as he realized he was traveling on one of the very roads of the old stories.

"We have stories in my land of people who came here," Arden said. "But..." he paused, "I just realized that I never understood why we stopped coming here. Do you know what happened?"

Ildera's face was very sad, and he said softly, "A great and terrible war took place. Then the road was abandoned. That was over a thousand year ago."

Arden was filled with sadness upon hearing this news, although he could not explain the depth of it.

"I will tell you now, so that you won't despair, that eventually we will leave the road and travel on a smaller path after we reach Lon. This path will not be easy to follow for someone who does not know the way. But I know the way and will guide you safely," Ildera said.

After fifteen minutes or so, they started out again down the road, and they spent the rest of the afternoon riding. Arden felt his leg muscles getting sore, and he was tired of the rain and gray clouds. He felt his head nodding once before he caught himself. Ildera might have sensed Arden's weariness, or maybe the timing was coincidence, but as Liberty slowed, Ildera motioned for Arden to look up ahead. In the distance, the clouds ended in a blue sky. The sight perked Arden up, and soon they were out of the rain. They stopped again to rest in the sun. Now that Arden could see the sky, he could tell it was definitely late afternoon.

"We're almost at the city," said Ildera. "We made good time. Thanks, old man," he said, patting Liberty. "We will come to a bridge that crosses a river before the city. When we get there, I will show you what I plan for us to do. We still need to hurry. The riders are still pursuing us, and they will not want to spend the night so close to the city."

So they rode on, and a short time later, perhaps less than an hour, they came to the bridge. The bridge was larger than Arden imagined. As they stood at the edge of it, Arden could see that a wide river formed a small gorge below, and looking to the right, it curved around until it almost made the other side look like an island. Giant pine trees lined the edge of the high bank. To the left, the river still curved, but the other bank was not as steep. Arden saw more old buildings there. The bridge was all stone, as far as Arden could tell, and they crossed it quickly. The road, angling to the left, was the way to the heart of the ruined city of Lon. Ildera bid Arden to dismount, and he led them through an old street to the right. At the end of the street, which appeared to be a dead end, a small path to the left led up a hill. The path ran straight and then cut back twice to give them a view of the city. They only had a moment's glance as Ildera wanted to continue quickly. Several paths branched from theirs, but they took a path that ran back towards the river. The path cut to the left and became wider. They continued until they reached a smaller path that branched off to the right. Ildera stopped and whispered something to Liberty. The horse continued down the trail, but Ildera motioned for Arden to follow him on this small path. Then he stopped and turned to Arden.

Speaking in a hushed voice, he said "We are going to the river's edge to wait for the pursuers and see what they will do. We need to be quiet. I doubt that they could hear us, but we don't want to take any chances, all right?"

Arden nodded, and they continued into a pine forest of huge trees. Arden could see by the brightness ahead that the edge was close. Slowing, Ildera led them to a spot overlooking the bridge. They were closer than Arden would have liked, but they lay on the ground behind some bushes where seeing them from the bridge with the sun behind them was impossible. Arden thought he heard something, and suddenly a rider in black appeared at the edge of the bridge. He was surprised that the queen's men were so close behind them, but Ildera did not react at all. Soon he could hear more horses, and then they appeared. They all stopped at the end of the bridge and did not cross.

The first rider said, "What do we do now, leader?" with a hint of sarcasm.

"Shut up, Tramus!" another man replied, probably the leader, Arden figured.

"Well, I'm not crossing into that accursed city," a third voice complained.

"You too," said the leader. Another group of five men came up behind them.

"Seen anything?" one of them asked.

"Nothing," said the one called Tramus. "I wonder if they even came this way."

"What about the horse tracks?" said the third man, scowling.

"Could have been there for days," said Tramus.

"Enough!" said the leader, who was clearly getting more aggravated by the second. "If they came this way, they either turned off the path or went into the city. Either way, they'll have to come back on this road to reach the crossroads. If they went into the city, they won't be coming back. So I suggest that we head back and camp as far back down this road as we can. We'll post a watch at the crossroads tomorrow and be back in Tyre by noon. Does anyone object to this plan?"

The men were silent. He continued, "Very well then. We'll start in five minutes."

The men drank water and ate quickly and went into the woods to relieve themselves. Unfortunately, Arden and Ildera did not move; so they had to listen to all of the cursing and foul language of the men. Finally, the soldiers rode away. Ildera still waited some time before he moved. If Ildera was listening to the horses, Arden could not tell, for he no longer heard them. Arden then wondered if what they had heard was all a show and maybe the men had not really left. Fear started to enter his mind. He finally had the nerve to move slightly and look at Ildera. Ildera's eyes were closed, and he seemed to be concentrating on something. Then he opened his eyes, looked at Arden, smiled, and then motioned for Arden to get up.

"That wasn't so bad, was it?" he said, starting down the path. "I'm sorry you had to listen to all that filth back there," he said. "It was necessary to wait until they were gone before we moved. They are an uncivilized lot, the outer guard. They were not from the queen's city, because there was not enough time to mobilize the official forces. It's well for us, though. The guards of Tyre hate to leave their city except to go to another city of their liking, not a trip to the wilderness. The legends of the forest scare them so badly that they justify their retreat by their fear. The queen will not be happy, but they will probably lie to her to escape her wrath."

"Are all the people of the land like those men?" asked Arden.

"No," said Ildera, "but many are, and the ones that aren't stray from the path more and more every day. But where we are headed, the people are not like those men. They are probably the closest people you could find to your own people. Eventually, when you reach Jeshuryn, you will find that the people there are close to you as well, in matters of the heart. But that city is still far away, and we need to make camp soon for the night."

Ildera and Arden continued along the smaller path and reached the larger path. Liberty was not there, but they followed the larger path away from the city. They continued down the path, which ran through a forest of pine trees. Their footsteps barely made any sounds, and Arden could not hear anything except birds chirping and Ildera humming slightly.

Ildera seemed pleased at the way things had happened. Finally, they came to an open field of tall grass. Arden saw that Liberty was up ahead, eating grass by a small stream. He neighed at the sight of Ildera and walked over to them as they approached. Ildera gave him a pat on the side and said words to him in a strange language. He laughed when he saw the confused look on Arden's face.

"Yes, I forget sometimes and speak the language of my youth. I was just telling him that we were successful and how glad I am to see him."

They continued on the path, which led back into another forest of pine trees, but they did not walk too much farther before they stopped for the day. Ildera seemed to be looking for a specific spot. They came to a small grove of tightly-packed trees and squeezed their way through an opening in the branches. The branches were just wide enough for Liberty to push through as well. The air was cool inside the clearing, and the light from the setting sun touched the tops of the trees far above. Obviously, Ildera had stayed here before. A small, wooden shelter and two wooded benches stood around a ring of stones where a fire could be lit. Near the shelter lay some dry wood with which Ildera started a fire. He unpacked a small tent and showed Arden how to set it up. The tent was for Arden to use. Ildera said that he mostly slept outside unless it was really cold or raining. Arden put his pack in the shelter, and he spread a blanket in the tent. Arden continued to build the fire while Ildera unloaded some supplies from Liberty. An iron pan hung on the outer wall of the shelter, and Ildera cooked some meat in it and served it with bread to Arden. A small hand pump connected to a well in the grove yielded water for them to drink. Next to the well was also a small trough from which Liberty could drink. Ildera had taken the packs off him, and Liberty stood silently nearby.

They did not say too much after supper. Before long, the night was dark, and the air was getting cold. But Arden felt relaxed near the warm fire after eating. The stars came out in the limited patch of night sky that they could see. Ildera told Arden that he would usually recite from the Scriptures after eating and then spend some time talking to the Lord Most High before going to bed. He suggested that they pray together, and tonight he said that he would make it short for Arden's sake. Arden was getting tired, and although he said nothing, his exhaustion was clear from his face. Ildera thanked the Lord Most High for guiding them safely that day and protecting them from harm. He thanked Him for protecting Hershel and his sons and the old woman and her grandchildren. The fire crackled now and then, and soon Arden had his chance to pray. Arden felt inside a feeling of great gratitude for having come this far on the trip without any major incidents. Words could not express his feelings, but he tried his best to say what he felt. The companions continued to pray, both silently and aloud, until a moment came when it seemed appropriate to stop.

Then they said good night, and Arden entered his tent. He took a few moments to get things organized and comfortable. Ildera put some more wood on the fire and then sat on the bench again. He stared up at the bright stars and began praying again. Arden fell asleep and slept so soundly that he did not even hear Ildera singing.

Chapter 13

The Path

The next morning, Arden woke hours after the sun rose. Ildera had been awake for some time but decided to let Arden sleep. Ildera warned him that this indulgence would not happen too often. Arden was more surprised when Ildera said that they would walk the rest of the way. He pulled Arden aside and said in a low voice, "Liberty is not as young as he used to be, and carrying us and all our gear is a burden to him." Arden was amused that Ildera spoke so that Liberty could not hear him.

"I know that you want to get to your destination as quickly as possible, but be patient. Besides, walking will do us good. You are not yet strong enough to cross the desert, and the walk will prepare you."

Ildera and Arden left the camp and walked under the tall pine trees. The path that they walked became wider, and a river appeared on the right. They walked for hours on this path beside the river. Occasionally, they would see the remains of old buildings. Ildera would talk about them as if they had been bustling with life last week. His descriptions were so detailed at times that Arden began to wonder how he could possibly know these things. The river suddenly turned sharply to the right, and the path they were traveling seemed to end. In front of them and to the right were marshes that stretched as far as Arden could see. To the left ahead rose what looked like hills and possibly mountains from the limited viewpoint that Arden had. Ildera did not seem concerned, and he and Arden walked through the woods, not really on any path until they came to a stone pillar. A new path continued from here which led uphill to the left. They continued for some time uphill, stopping for breaks a few times. Finally, the path joined an old road with grass growing on it. They followed this road for the rest of the day. The road was increasing in elevation, but Arden could not see anything to the right because of the trees. On the left were stone cliffs about twenty feet high, and at times the road seemed to be carved into the side of the hill. Finally, a field opened up to the left, and they turned onto it. Crossing it, they entered a grove of trees. To the right, Arden could see an open hillside with a view of whatever was out there, which he could not distinguish through the trees. He and Ildera made camp at the far end of the grove away from the open hillside. Ildera did not want to make a fire, and Arden, hot and tired, was not disappointed. They walked to the edge of the hillside and stood there as the sun set. Looking straight out, they could see a flat plain below. Mountains rose on the right and behind them to the left, but in front was desert as far as you could see. Ildera pointed out where the marshes ended and the desert began. The view was not spectacular, but seeing the desert, the first desert he had ever seen, filled Arden with curiosity.

"Is that the desert I need to cross?" Arden asked.

"Yes, it's the same desert, but we still have a way to go before we get to the right spot for the crossing. We are still too far east, and crossing would take far too long from here."

"What will the desert will be like?"

"It will be flat, hot, and dry. In many ways, though, it is no different than walking through the forest. The difference is in your mind. Crossing the desert takes a strong mind and will. Many men have died of thirst with water left in their bottle. They lacked discipline and self-control. More importantly, they lacked the Spirit of the Lord Most High to lead them, instead feeding on their fears and believing lies thrown at them." Seeing the distressed look on Arden's face, he added, "I do not believe that you will have that problem."

"How long will it take to cross?"

"You should need twenty days, and that estimate is with help. I cannot go with you, but I will make sure that another does. Do not worry."

Arden stood lost in thought. He could not imagine crossing such an expanse.

"Any other questions?" said Ildera jokingly. Arden hesitated. "Well, go ahead!" Ildera laughed.

"How old are you?" asked Arden.

"I think you are beginning to understand," said Ildera, chuckling, "I am one thousand, one hundred and forty-seven years old, give or take a few years. After a while, I lost track of some of the years. Yes, it's true," he said, seeing the surprised look on Arden's face. "I was born in the city of Korazin, one of the great cities of the plain." He motioned for Arden to sit. They sat on the ground, Ildera sitting with his back against a tree and Arden before him in the grass. The setting sun made the desert below seem like a vast sea of shining water, while behind Ildera the trees of the mountain were glowing with golden sunlight. The contrast was such that if Arden looked only at Ildera, he might never believe that a great desert was behind him.

"You may not know this, but the desert once contained a land filled with people in large cities with great wealth. The plains were fertile grounds covered with crops and animals. The people came from tribes that left Jeshuryn and settled there long before. At first, the plains dwellers kept strong ties with Jeshuryn, but as time went on, those ties diminished and were almost completely lost. We also lost our God, and we turned to money as a god along with many other gods. I grew up in this time of idolatry, and when I was young, I believed that I was in paradise. Now, the people themselves were not bad or evil, but their friendliness and their family ties lessened with each passing generation. But I did not know any of this history. My parents were wealthy, and my father was a leader in the city. I was skilled in reading and writing, and I developed an interest in planning layouts for new houses and public places. I designed a public park that was very popular, and I was starting to create a reputation for good, quality work.

"Then one day at a festival, I found myself greatly fatigued and not feeling well. I recovered for a while but began to have trouble breathing. My parents called in the best doctors, who tried all the remedies they knew, but nothing worked. Day after day I became worse, until finally I no longer had the strength to walk. I was bedridden, and no one could help me. My parents decided that maybe my illness was a matter for a higher power and summoned priests from the various temples where they worshipped. The priests came and prayed and danced and shouted. Later, they sprinkled me with water and blood and burned offerings to their gods. But each day, I still grew worse. One of the priests was very close to my parents, and he convinced them that I needed to be brought to his temple in another city. Of course, the priest was being paid well for his services. I think at first he really believed that I could be healed in his temple by the god he worshipped there. Instead, nothing happened except that the pain increased in my chest. Finally, the priest realized that I was not going to get better but that I was going to die. So he convened his inner circle. I can remember lying there, hearing those men discussing my fate, although they knew it not. They decided to have me secretly taken to the valley of Sorek, killed there, and my body dumped in the river. They would tell my parents that their god took me to heaven by a miracle. Of course, my parents would still have to pay offerings to this god to keep me there.

"So at night they took me. I was helpless; every breath had become an agony of pain. An elderly man and his son took me from the city on the back of a wagon. They placed bales of hay around me to keep people from seeing me. The journey took two days, and I don't know how I survived it. Many times, I passed out from the heat and the pain. The nights were cooler but humid, and the moisture made breathing more difficult. When the elderly man and his son reached the valley, they decided to dump me by the river. They were supposed to kill me first, but they did not. I'm not sure why. I suppose that they figured I was going to die anyway and they did not want my blood on their hands. I lay by the river all night until daylight came. And after the sun was up, I waited some time before some children found me. Thinking they had found a dead body, they stared at me in horror. But one child looked in my eyes and realized that I was alive. The children shouted loudly and then ran away. They were part of a group from Jeshuryn, making their way back to the entrance to their land. The elderly man must not have seen them from the wagon, or he would not have left me there. I still did not know if anyone would come to my rescue, if rescue was even possible. I lost consciousness and awoke at the sound of voices. I could not see his face clearly, but an old man with a white robe was standing over me. He had a staff, and I could see that he had a long beard. He was speaking words that I could not clearly understand, yet I could hear something powerful in the words. Although his voice was old, his words sounded young and alive. Others came and talked about what to do. They were speaking in their tribal dialect; I could hardly understand them. I think most of them wanted to leave me, but the old man demanded that they inquire of their God. He stood over me and mercifully blocked the hot sun, but no one would touch me. Others stood near him and joined in prayer. When they had finished, the man with the staff made a decree that I could not understand. Some went away quickly at his words. Two men came forward. They knelt beside me, and the old man knelt above my head. Those same men who left returned with something. It was water. The old man prayed aloud, and the two on the side joined him. I could make out some of the words. I thought that they were asking their God to heal me. I would have laughed had I been able to do so after what the other priests in the city had done, but despair had filled me. Then the men near me placed their hands on my chest, and I felt like fire was flowing from their hands: not a painful sensation, but like a cool burning. I could never explain it fully. Anyway, when they had finished, the pain was almost gone, and I could breathe easier. The old man lifted my head, and the other men gave me some water to drink. Never did water taste so sweet in my life! The old man bid me to rest, and some other men brought a litter and took me away.

Ildera paused for a moment in reflection. "I still can recall that journey to the gates of Jeshuryn. I was put inside a cool, dry tent when the travelers stopped and made camp for the evening. I could hear voices talking and later singing. Some of the songs stirred something inside me, and I felt my emotions rise with the excitement in their voices singing and then shouting. I realized that they were shouting praises to their God – the Lord Most High, the God that we plains dwellers had forgotten. Later, as the songs would get softer, peace would descend upon the camp, and I would fall asleep. During the day, the travelers sat me on a horse and bound me so that I would not fall. Riding in this manner was uncomfortable, but no more than what I had already endured. I wondered what these people would do with me. I was still weak and sick, and I did not know if I would live to reach the border or if the guards would let me in if I did. Strangers were not welcome anymore in Jeshuryn. On the other hand, looking back, I guess part of me knew that I would survive. I could feel a spark of hope returning to me, and life seemed to be returning to my body. Each evening, the old man with the staff would come in to visit me with his attendants. They would give me water, but I still could not eat. The old man would talk with me, asking questions about who I was and what my parents' names were. As my strength increased, each day I could tell him more. Each time he spoke to me, he would tell me that the Lord Most High had saved me and that He had a plan for my life. What could I say to such words? The fact that I was alive was a miracle.

"Finally, we reached the cliffs of the Lachmeth, the entrance to Jeshuryn. However, when we finally reached the gates, the guards would not let me pass. The guards were fearful because the old man was a great priest among their people, but I was a stranger that was sick and weak. For all they knew, I could have been carrying some disease. So they summoned the captain of the guard. He was in a dilemma. Here was a priest and leader who believed I should be allowed to enter the land, but the guard was under orders from the king not to admit any outsider without permission from the King of Kings. Again, I almost laughed. I had heard stories of the King of Kings as a child, but I thought he was a myth and not real. Things got tense for a moment, and then a trumpet sounded in the distance. A messenger from the City of Light, home of the King of Kings, was approaching. The messenger, a man on a brown horse, looked majestic in his gold helmet and uniform of red and gold. He gave the captain of the guard a message from the King of Kings, allowing me into the land and bidding me to come to the gates of the City of Light. Then, as quickly as he came, he turned and left. Silence fell. Then the priest and the captain of the guard made eye contact and started to laugh and rejoice. They hugged each other and made peace. The whole party and the guards celebrated that night, praising their God and the King of Kings. I could hear them through the window as I lay in a soft bed." Ildera stopped at this point and seemed lost in remembrance.

Arden waited patiently, but after some time he finally asked, "And then what happened?"

Ildera came back from his reverie and said, "I was taken to the city outside the City of Light. The King of Kings came and healed me." His voice was distant, for he was still lost in some thought.

"Is that why you lived so long?" Arden asked.

Ildera laughed. "No. That healing was only the beginning. I have much more to tell. However, seeing the desert again has filled my mind with memories and other thoughts; so now is not the time for me to tell that part of the story. We need to rest soon, for tomorrow will be a long day."

The next day, and for many days afterwards, Ildera and Arden continued on the path that led into the mountains south of the desert. They rose at sunrise, ate breakfast, and walked until noon. Then they would stop for lunch and a rest break. Sometimes Ildera would read and Arden would just lie in the grass or a comfortable spot. Other times Ildera would engage Arden in some practice sword fighting. Arden had some training, but was never really that interested in swordplay. Ildera was a true master of the sword who was patient with his teaching. His real passion, though, was teaching about the Scriptures. When they walked, he would teach Arden about them. Or course, Arden knew many of them because he had heard them, but he soon realized that he lacked the understanding of their application to life and their relevancy. He learned many things which he would recall later when needed. Every day, the food supply decreased as Arden's hunger increased from all the walking. Sometimes he woke up hungry in the middle of the night, but usually tiredness won out enough so that he returned to sleep.

Ildera and Arden reached a small clearing one afternoon, and Ildera stopped. He showed Arden the trees there, and Arden smiled when he saw that they were full of nuts. The men picked as much as they could carry and stopped there for the evening. Ildera taught Arden how to prepare the nuts. They needed to soak in water for at least an hour, and then they were boiled. As they boiled, the shells split and floated to the surface. The shells were scooped out and discarded, and the remaining liquid was thick and hearty, almost like gravy. It was surprisingly filling and had a pleasant taste. Ildera was glad Arden liked the food, because it would be their main staple for the next week. The sky had remained blue and the weather cool for most of their journey so far. The last week, though, brought rain every day. At first it was a gentle spring rain, but by the third day it was a steady rain.

The next morning, the men came to spot where the road seemed to end, and an opening in the shape of a circle was before them. Rain stopped falling for a moment, and the sun shone through. In the circle, grass grew around the ruins of stone pillars and the large slabs of rock in the center of them. On the other side was a large, stone archway with the stone figure of an angel on top. The angel had wings and was holding a sword and shield. He had a stern look on his face, which looked alive even though it was carved in stone. From the sides of the arches, a stone wall ran in a half circle, while behind the men were trees. They approached the arch, and Arden felt a powerful presence around them. He questioned Ildera.

Ildera explained, "We are entering Beriya. It is protected by the Lord Most High. No evil can enter through this gate. We have nothing to fear. Rather, I am thankful that we are here."

The men passed through the gate and entered Beriya. The road was clear and appeared to be well maintained. It ran flat and straight for the most part. The sky turned to gray again, and rain began to fall. Ildera and Arden continued walking, and Arden could begin to see signs that people lived here. Roads branched off here and there, and fences appeared now and then. The men stopped again for the night. By now, everything Arden had was damp or wet. His sodden state was a little discouraging, but Ildera reassured him.

"Tomorrow we will arrive at a place where we can spend the night indoors in a warm bed. We will stop at what I guess you would call a school. From there, we will go to the house of the keepers. The people here are friendly and kind, and they will welcome you openly. However, you would be wise not to speak of the purpose of your journey to everyone."

The next morning, rain was still falling, but the sky began to clear as Ildera and Arden turned off the road onto a smaller road that passed over a hill and opened into a valley in front of them. They passed by a field on the left and came upon a house with an old man sitting on the porch. He waved at them and bid them well. The travelers continued for a fair way and stopped for lunch. Then they continued on by fields and streams of water. Suddenly, the sun came out and shone brightly on the fields beside them on the left. Several roads branched off to the left, and now a wide field ran up a hill to the left. Before them was another field with the road running on the right. At the end of the field was a hill which was actually a dam with a small lake behind it. Arden and Ildera walked up the road to the right of the dam and down by the lake. To the right were red buildings. Arden walked down to the docks by the water. He lay down in the hot sun, which felt good to him. Ildera laughed. "You can stay here," he said. "I'll be back in a few minutes." Arden put his wet coat under his head and fell asleep.

Chapter 14

Beriya

Arden woke to the sound of laughter. He opened his eyes and saw a figure over him. A young girl was sitting by his head, smiling at him. He sat up and saw several boys and girls of different ages sitting on the benches to the left of him. A few more were coming down from the buildings behind. Some of the girls were looking at him and smiling, while the boys were gathered together on the far left. On the benches to the right, Ildera was sitting next to a young man. Sitting on the bench at the side of the dock was a young woman. She had long, brown hair and a pretty face. Standing next to her was a girl with blonde hair and a basket of small, white flowers in her hand. The girl was braiding the woman's hair and putting flowers into the braids. As Arden sat up, the woman laughed out loud and said, "I think Cassandra got some practice in, Lee," as she turned back to the man next to Ildera. He laughed out loud as well, and Ildera motioned to the puzzled Arden and mouthed "your hair" to him. Arden felt for his hair, one side of which was indeed braided. He could see white flowers in it. The child next to him just smiled and looked very pleased with the job she had done. She was five years old, and Arden found that he could not get mad at her.

"Don't worry," laughed the woman, "the flowers will come out in the water. And Eleanor will certainly cut your hair when she sees it." Most of older children laughed at that, as if from personal experience. Arden stood up and looked at his reflection in the water, and indeed, he did look extremely silly with one side braided with flowers. He almost laughed when he saw himself.

"Are we all here?" said the man. A count of heads confirmed that all the children were present. "You can go in the water now," he said. The kids ran down the dock and jumped into the water with glee. The older ones ran across the dock first, and then the younger ones followed.

The girl who had braided his hair, Cassandra, was still standing next to him. "Are you going into the water?" she asked. Arden looked at Ildera, who nodded his head in approval.

The water was cold after lying in the hot sun, but soon Arden was having as much fun as all of the other kids. They were all younger than he was, and he guessed that their ages were from five to eleven. The older boys swam to another dock across the water, while the younger kids went to a beach area on the right and played games in the sand and the shallow water. The older girls swam near the dock and spent more time talking than swimming. Before long, a whistle blew, and everyone swam to the beach and got out of the water. Towels were lined up on the fence for everyone. One of the older boys gave one to Arden. Everyone dried off and started walking towards the long buildings in front of them. The same older boy who had given Arden a towel, Jed, explained that they would get changed and then do their chores to help prepare for the evening. Arden was at a loss as to where to go. As the children came up the hill from the water, Arden could see down into the fields before the dam. A horse cantering there looked like Liberty, but Ildera was not riding him. The young man from the lake was. Standing in the field was Ildera and the woman with flowers in her hair. Arden left the boys, walked down to the field, and stood next to Ildera. The young man rode Liberty without a saddle, galloping up and down the field several times. Liberty seemed to enjoy this exercise, and the young man was having a lot of fun riding him. The young man turned and rode up to Ildera.

"I still love your horse," he said, laughing.

Ildera said, "So do I."

The woman said, "You should take him up to the barn now. You will have just enough time to get back here for the afternoon gathering."

"Of course, Miss," he said, bowing slightly. "He will be brushed, watered, and fed before then. By your leave," he said to Ildera.

Laughing, Ildera and the woman both just motioned for him to leave. The young man and Liberty turned and sped across the field.

"Arden, this is Jeveka, and that young man on my horse is Colley," said Ildera.

Arden turned to take Jeveka's hand, but she took him by surprise, giving him a quick hug and a kiss on the cheek instead. He was not displeased because she was very beautiful.

"Welcome to Beriya," she said. "A room should be prepared by now for you and one for Ildera. After swimming, we take a break to get changed. Then we will get ready for the evening meal. Let's walk back to the dining hall."

The three walked up the hill and entered the dining hall. An older woman there was setting the tables with the help of a few children. The youngest of the children were coming in after changing, and they were sitting in an adjacent room on a large rug in front of an older man named Jacob, who was resting on a chair. He was asking them questions, and Arden could see them raising their hands, waiting for him to call on them. The man was smiling, and the lesson looked like fun. Jed had come into the hall, and Jeveka asked him to show Arden and Ildera their rooms. She bid Arden to change quickly and return to the hall.

"You can help us in the lower fields," she said. "I will have Sierra bring you down."

Jed showed Ildera and Arden to their rooms. Arden liked the small room that Jed showed him. A comfortable-looking bed with a blue blanket over it filled one corner, and a desk stood in front of the one window by the door. A small dresser and night table were next to the bed. Clothes were laid out on the bed, and Arden found that they fit him nicely. He returned to the hall without difficulty or delay. A girl with blonde hair was on the other side by the door. He could tell that she must be Sierra by the way she reacted when she saw him. So he crossed the hall and met her by the door.

"Hi," she said, "you must be Arden. I'm Sierra. I'll take you down to the fields."

With that introduction, they went out the door. Arden walked with Sierra on the road that led down the hill in front of the lake with a long field of grass on their right. At the end of the field, a road led up a hill to the right. They continued straight on the road with fields of crops on their right and the forest on their left. They passed two boys carrying baskets of vegetables. The boys greeted them as they passed. Arden and Sierra did not enter these fields from which the boys had come but kept going. The road rose above the fields, curving first to the left and then to the right. Finally, Arden and Sierra turned down a small lane that ran to an iron gate, and beyond the gate was a garden of flowers and herbs. Jeveka was there with a basket in her hands, and she was picking some leaves and flowers. She stopped and smiled when she saw the new arrivals.

"Welcome!" she said. "This is our herb garden, and I am picking some seasonings for our supper. I thought you might enjoy this place. Sierra, get some of the black mint. We will give Arden a taste from the garden."

Sierra smiled as she left, and Arden suspected that the ladies were up to something. Jeveka continued through the garden and showed her guest many of the plants there. Some were familiar to Arden, and some were not. Sierra came back with some small, black leaves in one hand and a small, white berry in the other.

"Arden, are you brave?" asked Jeveka with a smile.

"I think so," he said hesitantly. Sierra laughed.

"We have something for you to try. Take the black leaves and put them in your mouth. Chew them as much as possible for as long as you can. Then Sierra will give you the white berry. Put it in your mouth, but wait a minute before you chew it. We will watch, and probably laugh," she said.

Arden took the leaves, put them in his mouth, and started to chew them. The taste was sour and bitter and strong for such small leaves. The expression on his face must have been funny, because the ladies laughed at him. Finally, he could not stand the taste, and Sierra gave him the berry. Instantly, his mouth tasted sweet but had some bitterness left. They told him to chew the berry slowly, and he did. The taste was amazing, indescribable, and joyous. The ladies stood watching, approvingly. When the taste subsided, the three talked more as they headed back to the buildings. Supper was cooking, and Jeveka added the appropriate herbs to the right pots. During a brief free time between chores and dinner, the boys and a few girls were outside watching Colley and Ildera practice with wooden swords. Colley was very good but no match for Ildera. Ildera would stop at certain points and teach his opponent some new skill. The boys were awestruck. Arden was about to go outside and watch, but Eleanor caught him and insisted that she should cut his hair. So the remaining children inside saw Eleanor's skill with scissors.

Everyone ate a hearty meal, and Ildera and Arden were most appreciative of it. This evening was a special one at the end of the week, and the inhabitants of the school spent it playing games, singing, and listening to stories, ending the evening in prayer. While the children were being put to bed, Ildera and Arden walked outside. The moon shone so brightly that they were able to see clearly down the road. They turned to the right and went up a hill. They had not walked for very long before they came to a small clearing on the right. In the middle, a small fire was burning, surrounded by benches. Ildera added wood to the fire and tended it. "Soon Jeveka, Colley, Eleanor, and Jacob will come," he said.

"What will we do?" asked Arden.

"We will sing and talk and laugh, I hope," laughed Ildera. "We are blessed to have such people here at this time. You see, Jeveka and Colley are betrothed, and they will eventually become the king and queen of this land. They both care deeply for their people, and they are strong and brave. Jeveka is very good at reading people, and the Spirit of the Lord Most High is with her. She has a passion for healing and hates to see anyone in distress. She is known to see into the future what the Spirit of the Lord Most High reveals." Soon the others came, and they all spent an enjoyable evening under the stars. When they were praying, Arden could feel the powerful presence of the Spirit of the Lord Most High. He looked up and saw Jeveka staring at him. She came over and sat next to him, taking his hand. She did not say anything, but he felt that she was staring straight through him to his heart. He could feel the love radiating from her, not a romantic pull, but the love of the Lord Most High. Then she got up and sat back next to Colley. Arden did not see the tears in her eyes.

Chapter 15

The Keepers

Arden and Ildera left the hall after breakfast and some hearty farewells. A trail ran from the side of the hall up the hill, which led to the same dirt road that ran past the fields. The trail was a shortcut which led them over a small ridge by the stream that ran into the lake. When they reached the road, they turned left. Nothing but forest was on the left, and several side paths led off from the road now and then. To the right were also woods, which did not go too far. When Ildera and Arden reached a clearing, Arden could see that they were on the edge of a much larger ridge. They had stopped for a moment, and Ildera walked over to the edge with Arden to see the view. They were looking down into a small valley where they could see part of a road at the bottom. The ridge on the other side ran parallel to theirs, but they seemed like they would meet up ahead. Arden could not tell how far that intersection would be. Ildera and Arden walked at a slower pace, although Ildera seemed both excited and impatient to reach their destination. The morning was beautiful, and walking in the cool breeze with a crystal clear blue sky overhead was relaxing. Finally they came upon a stone wall on the right that was at least ten feet high and had vines overhanging it. The wall went on for some time until they reached an entrance. The travelers passed through the stone archway into a small courtyard with a small fountain in the middle. Ildera and Arden were at the side entrance of the house of the keepers. To the left was a solid stone wall which ended with a small staircase and entrance to the house. To the right was another, much shorter wall. A row of pine trees blocked any view. Straight ahead and to the right was another gate. Ildera and Arden walked towards the gate, through which a cool breeze was blowing. As if on cue, an older man came through the arch and spoke.

"Ah, it's about time you got here," he said, motioning for the men to follow him.

Arden did not see the smile on Ildera's face because he was beginning to see a glimpse of what lay ahead beyond the gate. He stopped in awe at the view when he went through the gate. The whole landscape opened up, and Arden felt like he was standing on the edge of the world. Below, full of trees and plants, were a series of terraces that seemed to drop off suddenly. In the distance on the right were huge mountains. Straight ahead and to the left far below were empty plains that stretched as far as the eye could see. A stone path ran to the right diagonally to the gate, with another small, stone wall on the right. Ildera had gone ahead along the path that led to an open area where Arden saw a table and chairs. Ildera greeted the man and embraced him wholeheartedly. The men laughed when they saw the astonished look on Arden's face, and Ildera bid him to join them. Arden felt almost dizzy for a moment at the view, but he quickly joined Ildera and the older man, who greeted him.

"My name is Eleazar, and I welcome you in the name of the Lord Most High," he said, embracing Arden. "You will find a washroom through that door," he said, pointing. "My wife will join us momentarily with tea and food; so go and refresh yourselves." Ildera led the way, and he and Arden were back in no time. "Please, sit down," said the man. Four cups were on the table next to a large pot of tea. A woman emerged from the house carrying a tray. She was older as well, and she smiled when she saw Ildera.

"Welcome back, Ildera," she said as she put the tray on the table. Ildera stood and embraced her, and she kissed his cheek. "It's been far too long since you have been here," she said.

"I agree," said the man.

"And you must be Arden," she said as she walked around the table towards him. He stood in politeness, and she surprised him by warmly embracing him and kissing him on the cheek as well. "You are also welcome here."

"Indeed," said the man.

They spoke for awhile, but Arden was not really listening. Most of the conversation was about people and places that he did not know. Finally, Prisca, Eleazar's wife, graciously asked him if he wanted a tour. He readily agreed. She brought him down the stairs of the front terrace, where Arden walked slowly. He kept looking out with the feeling that he would end up far below if he fell. Prisca laughed and said that getting used to the height took some time. Then she explained what this place was.

"Once, the desert was full of life, until the day that the people deserted the Lord Most High. He declared that the land would become a lifeless desert and remain so until the appointed time. A remnant of us still served the Lord Most High, and we brought as many plants as we could here to save them. The Spirit of the Lord Most High caused many others to grow here. Yes, I am one of the old ones, as we are called, like Ildera. But our job is to tend these plants until the day we can return to our former land. So we are called the keepers."

Arden and his hostess spent most of the afternoon walking though the various levels. Prisca was a wealth of information, and Arden was amazed at her knowledge. As they approached the bottom of the lower terrace, they stopped for a moment. The valley on the right narrowed as it approached the narrow lip in front of them. From there, the side became a cliff to the edge of desert far below. Directly in front of them was an oval-shaped area with trees that were planted in dirt. A wall of stone surrounded them with a parapet on which you could walk. Prisca explained that all of the waste from the house, the barns, and the gardens ran through pipes down into the circle below. Despite this system, only a sweet fragrance filled the air. In the center of the circle grew a large tree, one of the largest in the gardens.

"This tree is the Izsasko tree, one of the best and the worst of all the plants in the garden. Because it thrives on waste, long ago most houses had one planted nearby. Something in the roots eliminates the smell of waste, and when the leaves fall, they can be carried away and used as fertilizer. In the spring and summer, pink blossoms will bloom, and the tree produces small, red fruit. The fruit is a poison which is merely left to fall on the ground. Another tree similar to this one produces a fruit that contains an addictive drug with many bad side effects. The two were crossbred, and the result was even worse: a fruit that produced vile behavior and sterility in women who used it. A beautiful tree, but deadly." She paused, as if to choose her words carefully, for she could tell that Arden would not understand the depths of the behavior the hybrid fruit caused. The blossoms were not open, perhaps because of the overcast sky, but a deep fragrance hung heavy in the air. It was almost sickeningly strong.

"The Queen has an orchard of these trees, and they are well guarded. She destroyed the rest of them so that she would have complete control. This tree is the only other one known to exist. She refines the fruit into a potent liquid which she uses for her, um, festivals. Unfortunately, this tree is a hybrid as well. Someday, when the land is restored, I know that the Lord Most High will restore it to the way it was."

Arden found the fragrance overpowering and felt ill.

"Are you all right?" asked Prisca.

"I feel lightheaded and sick to my stomach," Arden said.

Taking him by the arm, Prisca quickly led him away. "Let's make our way back along this path, for more things here will interest you." They walked for a minute and came to some benches where they sat. Some water flowed nearby, and Prisca took some for Arden to drink. Before she gave it to him, she found a tree with small bunches of orange flowers, and she picked a small branch with flowers on it. She stirred the flowers in the water and then gave it to Arden. Once he drank the water, he felt better. The flowers gave the water a slightly sweet taste of lemon.

Arden and Prisca headed back up to the house and ate supper there. Arden was tired, and he went to bed early. The other three, who had much to talk about, stayed up quite late.

With Prisca's consent, Arden spent most of the next morning in the east garden, tending to the plants and exploring a bit. He had gotten over his fear of falling over the edge in the steep parts. Unseen from the house was a valley to the right, through the bottom of which a small stream bubbled. A fairly good-sized lawn bordered both sides of the stream and another whole section of gardens he had not seen. The gardens were much more extensive than he had thought, and the variety of plants fascinated him extremely. Around midmorning, Prisca found him and brought him tea and cakes that she had made. They sat at a little table in the shade. Jeveka was with her, and she and Arden left to explore some more.

Jeveka and Arden walked on the wall at the very edge of the lowest terrace. He was able to look over the edge and see the steep sides that led down to the desert below. Jeveka pointed out some of the mountains in the distance and told Arden their names. Then she pointed far to the left, where the path across the desert was. Even from this height, they could not see the mountains at the edge of Jeshuryn. The sun was overhead, and Arden felt that he could stay still for a long time and be content just to look. However, he and Jeveka needed to get back for tea so that Prisca would not be disappointed. As they turned to go, a strong wind came down from the right and stirred up a storm of pollen from the Izsasko tree. The pollen hit Arden full in the face, and he breathed it in. It stung his eyes, which began to water. The sweet fragrance was overwhelming, and he felt a strange burning inside. Jeveka had turned her head, and when she turned back, she laughed at first because the white pollen looked like snow in Arden's hair. He had a strange look on his face, and his eyes were so bloodshot that they could hardly stay open. He took a step and staggered, grabbing the wall for support.

"Are you all right?" asked Jeveka. He turned and fell to the ground. Jeveka overcame her shock and dragged him from the wall up the steps to the next level, where the chance of another pollen-laden wind was less likely. Arden was speaking incoherently and laughing to himself. "Arden! Arden!" said Jeveka, but her efforts to recall him were of no use. He did not seem to hear her. "Spirit of the Lord Most High, I need your help," she said. Turning to face the terraces above her, she called for help. Her voice was piercingly loud, and she knew it would reach the others. Colley and Ildera were practicing some sword moves when they heard the call. Both of them ran down the stairs immediately.

Jeveka's call had brought Arden back to the present. Jeveka was kneeling by his head, praying. Arden was not laughing anymore, and the rush of fever that had overcome him dissipated, leaving him cold and shaking. "Jeveka," said Arden, "you are the most beautiful woman I have ever seen. I love you. But I love Sarah more." Jeveka opened her eyes in surprise, but Arden had drifted back into semi-consciousness again. Ildera and Colley found Jeveka and Arden in no time. Jeveka told them what had happened, and Ildera carried Arden back to the house of the keepers. Colley ran ahead to tell Eleazar and Prisca what had happened. Ildera brought Arden to the garden at the side of the house and laid him on a recliner. Prisca came out with a tray of bottles, and Eleazar carried two buckets of water and towels. Jeveka had followed behind and now was at the garden as well. Prisca set the tray on the table and opened several bottles. She dumped their contents into one bucket of water and threw a towel in as well. Taking the soaking wet towel, she wiped Arden's face and eyes, although Ildera and Colley had to hold each of Arden's arms down in restraint.

"What are you doing to me?" asked the half conscious Arden. He kept saying random things and meaningless words, sometimes laughing.

Once his eyes were washed, the redness slowly cleared. "Now for the inside," said Prisca. She took a teacup, filled it partway with water from the bucket, and took a small blue vial from the tray. She pulled the stopper off and added three drops to the cup. A fragrance filled the air from just the three drops that smelled like clover, hay, and mint. She made Arden drink the liquid, and his body twitched after he swallowed. His rambling became less frequent, and in a few minutes he stopped talking altogether. His eyes, however, remained distant, and he did not seem to be aware of his surroundings. The keepers exchanged an unhappy look. Then Prisca took another bottle containing a yellow liquid and put a few drops in the cup with some water. A very subtle scent of lilies filled the air. She made Arden drink this tincture as well. Almost immediately, his eyes came back into focus, and he saw his five companions standing over him. Ildera and Eleazar were still praying for him. Jeveka and Colley were staring, somewhat wide-eyed.

Arden sat up and for a minute remained silent, as if he was trying to make sense of everything.

"Arden," said Prisca, "you're back with us now. The dreams are over. Let them go; they were not real. Look at us and see."

Arden looked up at them. "Yes, you're right," he said. "What happened to me?"

"The pollen from the Izsasko tree overwhelmed you," said Prisca. "I should have told you not to go near it again."

"Ildera, Colley, why don't you bring Arden over to the eastern cabins? He can rest in there for now," said Eleazar. Ildera and Colley helped Arden to his feet.

"Make sure he drinks plenty of water," said Prisca as they went away. When they were out of hearing range, she said to Eleazar, "This incident is very unfortunate." He looked equally as grim. To Jeveka she said, "Tell me, child, exactly what happened, and everything he said."

Chapter 16

The Test

Arden slept all of the afternoon. When he awoke, he was in a different building, but he could see the house of the keepers and started back towards it. Arden came to the terrace outside the house. He stood there for a few minutes, enjoying the view. He turned towards the house to see if the others were around. As he approached the house, he could hear raised voices.

"None of us have had to take the test," said Colley.

"It will weaken him for the crossing," said Jeveka.

"It will make him stronger when the time comes," said Eleazar.

"But the cost is high," Jeveka replied.

"Have you seen what he will see?" asked Prisca.

"I have only seen a portion of what might happen," said Jeveka.

"We don't have the right to do this," said Colley.

"Ildera is responsible for him. Has he not agreed that this test is the right thing to do?" said Prisca.

"But it seems so cruel!" said Jeveka.

"He does not have to partake. Have you not thought that he might withstand the temptation? Or have we spoken doubt and unbelief in our friend? The decision has been made, and the discussion is over," said Eleazar.

"But it's my fault. I should be punished," said Jeveka.

"Foolish child, what's done is done, and there is no sense in our punishing you or you punishing yourself. It was an accident," said Eleazar.

Colley and Jeveka came out of the house and looked surprised to see Arden there. Colley looked sad, and Jeveka had tears streaming down her face. She threw her arms around Arden and embraced him firmly. Then she took a step back, still holding his shoulders. Colley stood next to him and put his hand on Arden's back. Jeveka embraced him again and then kissed him on the cheek.

"Remember that we love you," she said, and then they left.

Ildera came out from the house.

"What's going on?" asked Arden.

Ildera replied "I'm afraid that, because of your exposure to the pollen, the keepers would like you to undergo a ritual test that has not been done in a very long time. It is possible that the next time that you are exposed, if ever, you could become extremely addicted. You know about the drug that the queen makes. The keepers want to make sure that she can never use it against you."

"What do I have to do?" he asked.

"The test is more about what you have to resist doing. The tree produces fruit, and one from this tree has already ripened. We will put the fruit in a cup in the same room with you for one night. All you have to do is not eat the fruit. Resist the temptation, and you'll be fine."

"What if I eat it?" Arden asked.

"I don't know. Everything depends on how your body reacts. I think that you are strong enough to resist the temptation. The keepers will know what to do otherwise."

"When is this test going to happen?"

"We will leave now. We have a good walk to the place we're going."

Ildera led Arden down a path to the left past the steep terraces. The path led down a long series of steps and then up another set, winding around several corners until it came to several courtyards. These courtyards did not seem like part of the terraces with many plants but an area that was more manicured, composed of small lawns and patios adorned with statues and fountains. The men passed through one of the courtyards and then turned into a small garden on the left with a black iron gate. It had stone walls on three sides that were at least twenty feet tall. A fountain pattered musically on the right with a small chair and table behind it. A reclined seat on the left with a blanket on it almost looked like a bed. Most prominently displayed in the center of this area was a black pillar of stone. On top of the pillar was a round dish that was also stone and part of the pillar. In the dish was a red ball. When Ildera and Arden came closer, Arden realized, not only by sight but by the perfumed smell, that the ball was the red fruit from the Izscaso tree.

"Well," said Ildera, "I must leave you now. I have to lock the gate so that you will not be able to leave until morning. If I were you, I would make myself comfortable and get some sleep. The night will be dark in a while." He showed Arden where a small bathroom was on the far wall, and then they walked to the gate. Ildera closed the gate and locked it from the other side. "Remember," he said, "you do not have to eat the fruit. You can resist the temptation. The Spirit of the Lord Most High will help you if you ask His aid. I will be back in the morning."

After Ildera left, Arden walked around the perimeter, but he did not find much new to see. Probably an hour of light was left before the night became dark. He lay on the recliner, which was comfortable. The evening was not yet quite cool enough to use the blanket, but he put it on anyway.

This is not so bad, he thought. *I can easily do this.* He closed his eyes and started to relax. But as he did, the smell of the fruit seemed to get stronger. It made him feel sick, as he thought of the tree. Yet more and more the desire to look at the fruit filled his mind, and its smell was fragrant, not over-whelming like the tree had been. He thought about moving the recliner farther away from the pillar, and he tossed and turned for thirty minutes, wrestling with the thought of the fruit. Finally, he got up. He walked over to the pillar to look at it. The pillar was polished stone, and the orange sky gave it a strange glow. The fruit did not look red but almost black in the light. The sweet smell was stronger and the desire to touch it overwhelming. A voice in the back of his mind was pleading with him to walk away and let it go.

Instead, Arden grabbed the fruit and took a bite. His mouth exploded with a sweet flavor that was even better than the smell. He greedily ate the rest of the fruit. Almost immediately, after the taste subsided a bit, he felt a surge of energy in his body. Suddenly he felt like every nerve had become energized. The sensation was not painful but exhila-rating. He wondered why he must be confined when he felt this good. He looked around him and saw the very tips of the plants on the terrace above. He decided that he could climb the wall easily, and he started towards it. Halfway there, he turned towards the iron gate and stopped. Surely he could easily break the gate open instead. He started over towards it. Halfway to the gate, he heard a bird call from beyond the walls behind him. He turned and thought how easily he could run and jump over the wall, flying like a bird. Several more times these thoughts assailed him, each distraction turning him around so that he was walking in a circle. Then his head started to spin, and he felt dizzy. He hardly felt the dizziness as he fell backwards onto the grass and stared up at the sky. He laughed out loud when he realized what had happened. This feeling was not the terrible experience that he had expected. He no longer felt energetic but relaxed, and he had a feeling of incredible goodness about him. The dizziness was slowly fading. He was surprised when the light of the sky vanished and the night was suddenly dark. He didn't even realize that he was no longer conscious.

As he looked into the darkness, he could barely discern a pattern. The shape seemed so familiar, but he just could not figure out what it was. Gradually he started to feel the rest of his body, and he realized that he was holding onto something. It felt like a handle. Slowly he became aware that he was face to face with a large, wooden door. His forehead was literally touching the door. The pattern was the grain in the wood. For a moment, he thought he was lying on the door, but he managed to push the handle down and open it. The door opened into the back of a large church. As he walked forward, he could see that the pews were full of people, although he could not distinguish any distinct person. At the front of the church, a service was in progress. He started to walk down the center aisle, an action which should have felt awkward, but wasn't. None of the people he passed seemed to notice him at all. He still could not see any details, and he didn't try. His eyes were fixed on the altar. He could now see that the service was a wedding ceremony. The bride and groom were facing the priest as he was reciting the marriage vows. Arden kept walking closer and closer to the front. The bride and groom turned to face each other just as he was at the very first row. He felt shock like ice water hitting him in the face when he saw that the bride was Sarah. He wanted to say something, but he couldn't. Then she turned, looked right at him, and said, "I'm sorry Arden; I just couldn't wait." Then she turned to kiss the groom. Arden tried to move forward, but strong arms restrained him. He tried to speak, but he couldn't. He tried to turn away, but he couldn't leave either. Whoever or whatever was holding him would not let him move. He looked down at the floor, anything to avoid seeing

Sarah kissing another man. Then the arms let him go, and he fell onto the wooden floor.

As soon as he hit the floor, he looked up and saw that he was no longer in the church but on a raft in the middle of the sea. The sun was hot, and the air seemed stuffy. The raft was just an eight-foot-square flat area with no handhold to steady him. As the waves rolled and the raft pitched, he found himself struggling to stay on it. He rolled towards the left side and immediately tried to crawl the other way. Another wave picked up the raft, and it came crashing down almost vertically into the trough of the waves. As the raft came down, he was thrown forward, only to land on top of a sand dune. He stood up and found himself in the middle of a desert under a bright full moon. As the wind gently blew sand off the dunes in the distance, he started to feel cold. The wind began to pick up and blow sand in his face. At the same time, the sand dunes started to move like the waves of an ocean. He lost his footing and fell down the side of a dune face first into the sand. He got sand in his mouth, and he felt like he swallowed some. His stomach was upset, and his mouth had a bitter taste in it. More and more sand seemed to be blown into his mouth, which felt dry and gritty. The more he could taste the bitterness, the more upset his stomach became. Before too long, he was vomiting, in the vision as well as in reality. He felt like he was vomiting sand. His stomach hurt, and he realized that he was continuing to dry heave. Sweat poured from his forehead as chills ran through his body. The blowing sand stopped and was replaced by a cold, damp fog. He stopped dry heaving and lay down on the ground, which felt like snow beneath him, or maybe wet peat. He didn't care as long as the pain stopped. The night got dark, and he seemed to lose all track of his surroundings.

He heard the sound of water splashing next to him. Although his body was cold, his head was hot, and his forehead was sweating. He felt a wet cloth gently pat his brow and heard the water splash again as it was being wrung out. He opened his eyes, and the first thing he saw was a woman's face. He found himself lying on a reclining couch with his head in her lap. She had greenish brown eyes and blonde hair. On top of her head was a gold tiara. She was wearing a pink robe with intricate designs on it. She had a gold necklace and gold rings on her fingers. But her most noticeable feature at present was her face. It seemed perfect. No imperfections were visible. Her startling beauty was hard to describe. She was beautiful, but not like Sarah. He could not explain why.

"There, there," she said gently, "all this trouble because you would not come through my kingdom. I am the Queen about which you have heard so much. What a shame that you will die in the desert alone. Your two companions were much wiser in their choices. See, look for yourself."

She sat him up, and he could see Lavin and Marcus sitting nearby. Each was sitting, richly dressed, on a reclining chair. Marcus had black leather boots and a matching vest. Lavin had a brown robe with a golden belt and leather sandals. Both men had a cup in their hand and two women each on either side attended them. He was surprised to see his fellow exiles in such an honored position. The Queen had her arm around his shoulders and held him firmly and reassuringly. Another man occupied a third seat. Well built and tan, he wore an open red shirt, baggy black pants, and sandals. He had a gold crown on his head. He appeared to be interested only in two girls that sat before him, both mesmerized by his smile and charm. Behind and above them on a platform were two thrones.

The Queen spoke again. "And to think that all of this fuss started because you sat on a throne: after all, it's only a chair." She took him by the hand and led him to the thrones. "This is my throne and the throne of the king. Dearest," she said to the third man, "can Arden sit upon your throne?" The man gave a brief nod and a wave of his hand as if he could not have cared less. "Why do you think the King of Kings doesn't let anyone else sit on His throne? He wants you to obey Him blindly. He is afraid that you will find out that you don't need Him." As she was saying these words, an attendant appeared with a white robe, which the Queen put on Arden. She sat him in the king's throne and put a crown on his head. She looked approvingly at him and said, "Ladies, what do you think of him?" Two attractive female attendants appeared and knelt before him.

"He's so handsome," said one of them, smiling playfully.

"I'll do anything for you," said the other.

"Hail, King Arden!" the Queen cried, and everyone in the room cheered.

The vision faded, and Arden was back in the garden again. Somewhere in a distant room was the sound of cruel laughter. A voice said, "A seed has been planted."

Arden woke up the next morning with a terrible head-ache. He was lying on the bed, although he did not remember how he got there. His mouth was dry and tasted terrible. A light blanket lay over him to keep him warm. Next to the bed was a small table with a cup on it. A note in front of the cup read, "Drink this; you will feel better - I". He sat up painfully and realized that his entire body ached. Taking the cup, he put it to his lips. He was not sure he could drink it, for even though he was thirsty, his stomach felt queasy. The liquid in the cup looked like water, but it had an earthy smell. He took a sip and let it hydrate his mouth before swallowing. The coolness felt good going down his throat. He drank the rest of the liquid and leaned back on the bed with his eyes closed. He heard the sound of birds singing in the distance. The sun was rising, and the coolness of the night would end soon. As the thoughts of last night returned, he felt a sense of shame at giving into the temptation and eating the fruit despite the warning. Would Ildera and the keepers think less of him? Then he felt a sinking in his heart as the part of the vision with Sarah came into remembrance. He missed her more than ever and despaired at the thought of losing her. His heart ached, and his mind was troubled. Slowly he felt the liquid he drank counter the effects of the fruit. A poison, Prisca had called it. The fog in his mind began to clear, and he sat up. He would have liked to stay in this bed, but he felt compelled to get up. The gate was open, for the test was over.

He walked back along the path and up the stairs, trying to remember the way he had come. However, he took a wrong turn somewhere and was lost. His wrong position was easy to tell because the house of the keepers was far above on the left when it should have been on the right. Yet he continued in the same direction for some reason. *Am I still in the vision?* he thought. But his heart said *no, this is real.* He followed a set path although he did not know why; it just seemed the right way to go. A small pavilion stood on a hill to the right, and the morning sun was shining on it. He made his way to it. There he found chairs with cushions on them and a round table in the middle with books on it. He sat in a chair in the sun, and the warmth of the sun felt good on his face. In his heart, though, he felt guilty, dirty, and shamed for giving in without even the smallest fight. And he had not called upon the Spirit of the Lord Most High to help; he had assumed he could resist all on his own. "I'm so stupid," he said quietly, "Lord, I need You. I failed You. How can I get across the desert without You?" He sank into despair, and tears welled in his eyes.

"There's no point in torturing yourself over it," said a man's voice. "What's done is done, and it's time to move on." Arden looked up to see a man standing nearby. He was not surprised, though, for somehow he knew that someone was there. For a second, he thought this man was the king of Caladen, but he was not. Yet the man had an authoritative presence about him.

"Who are you?" Arden asked.

The man replied "I am a teacher. I come here sometimes to teach people."

"What do you teach them?" he asked.

"I teach them mostly about themselves," said the man. As he said this he looked at Arden and it felt like his gaze went all the way into the depths of Arden's heart.

"Oh," said Arden softly.

The man sat down across from Arden. "Why don't you tell me about your troubles?"

At first Arden was reluctant to admit his wrongdoing, but as he started to speak, he found it easier to tell about the test and then the visions. Even the part about Sarah came out without difficulty, and he felt like he was unloading the pain from his heart. The man did not a say a word or ask a question while Arden was speaking. When Arden finished, he felt like a great weight had been lifted from his heart, although sorrow and doubt remained.

"Are you truly sorry for giving in to temptation?"

"Yes."

"Then ask the Lord Most High for forgiveness, and you will receive it."

Arden bowed his head and asked for forgiveness. When he was through, the man continued. "Now, as far as the Queen is concerned, she has sold out to her master, the father of lies. If you believe in her words, you will die in the desert, but if you believe in God's words, you will live. Did not Prisca tell you that the fruit was dangerous to consume? It most always opens the door for some evil to get through. I would say that nothing you saw was real. The Spirit will help you to understand." He stood and motioned towards the path. "Now if you follow that path over there which leads up those stairs, you will eventually come back to the house of the keepers. If you go now, you can meet them outside the house before they go searching for you. Peace be with you, Arden; the Lord Most High is with you."

Arden left and followed the path that the man had indicated, and he never thought to ask how this man knew his name.

Chapter 17

Farewells

A rden reached the house as the others were about to search for him. They seemed overjoyed to see him, and Jeveka rushed to embrace him. The rest followed in turn. They did not ask any questions but headed back to the place where they first entered the house.

"I am afraid that the time has come for you to leave us," said Eleazar, and there was a touch of sadness in his voice.

"Yes," said Prisca, "we are sad because we have so much that we could teach you. But we trust in the Spirit of the Lord Most High, and we know that now is the time for you to go. Before you leave, we have some things for you."

A table was set up on the lawn in front of them. Six cups were on the table with a pitcher next to them. Prisca filled the cups with a golden liquid. The smell was sublime, with the faint peppery hint of marigolds, but the flavor was indescribable, like summer captured in a taste. The drink brought a sense of joy to his heart. Jeveka laughed as she watched his face.

"Yes. It tastes like that for us, too," she said. "The drink is from a fruit that only blossoms once in a great while. It is the perfect cup of farewell."

As she said these words, a sense of sweet sorrow filled Arden at the thought of leaving them, and the taste was like autumn with the leaves falling against the evening sky.

"Come here," said Eleazar, motioning for Arden to join him. "This is my gift to you. It is a sword from long ago, and it is light and strong. The man who owned it was honorable and greatly respected. He bid me to give it away some day to someone worthy to carry it."

Arden took the sword, which was amazingly light. He drew it from its scabbard and saw that the metal was intricately carved with words that he could not read.

"They are Scriptures," said Ildera, "and I will translate them for you someday."

Prisca gave Arden a package wrapped in paper. "Inside this package are twenty small cakes, made by Jeveka." Jeveka blushed slightly at this acknowledgement. "They will help sustain you as you cross the desert. Each one may appear small, but is enough to sustain you for an entire day. Be wise in your management of them."

Arden bowed to the keepers and said, "I thank you with all my heart for your hospitality."

"You are welcome to return any time," said Eleazar. "Now go with the peace and blessings of the Lord Most High."

Eleazar and Prisca hugged Arden again before he left. Arden, Ildera, Jeveka, and Colley went back to the school again. The children there were happy to see them again. By now, it was late afternoon, and they walked down to the field so that Ildera could see Liberty as the children did their chores. Jeveka and Colley went to do theirs as well. Liberty galloped towards Arden and Ildera and stopped abruptly in front of Ildera. He nuzzled Ildera and even Arden a bit.

"What will we do now?" he asked.

"We will leave tomorrow morning. We still have a considerable walk before we reach the edge of the desert."

The next morning, Arden and Ildera bid farewell to the children, Jeveka and Colley, and Eleanor and Jacob. As Ildera was coming back soon, this farewell was really Arden's. Ildera and Arden ate breakfast first and then said goodbye. The children all gave Arden hugs, and the girls gave him a gold and green bandana that they had made. The boys gave him a rope that they had made. Ildera commented that the children were instructed to give him practical things. Arden was grateful and thanked them. He and Ildera went outside, where Colley said farewell. He gave Arden a ring to wear on his finger. The ring was made of gold, and it had a cross symbol on it. Arden thanked him. Finally, Jeveka embraced him with a tear in her eye.

"My farewell gift to you is words," she said. "The Scriptures tell us to guard our hearts, for out of them life flows like water. [11] May the grace and peace of the Lord Most High be with you."

With the sadness of parting, Arden and Ildera turned and walked on the road that led across the dam and out towards the path that would lead them down to the desert. At a distance, they turned around to wave again, for the others had walked down behind them across the dam and stood there watching. Out of the wind came a voice, Jeveka singing:

I danced on the new grass
That came in the spring,
And sang in my garden with love.

A flower bloomed there
The purest white
In the light of the sun from above.

But I ran away and left it there
To dance on the shores of the sea,
And when I returned, the flower I loved
Was no longer there for me.

So I walked through the land
With my heart filled with sorrow,
And I had no desire to sing.
I walked up high on the mountain,
And there I met the King of Kings.

Then the sadness inside turned to joy;
Why should I weep and mourn?
Another season will surely come,
And another flower will be born.

The travelers rounded a corner and were out of sight. Arden was puzzled by the song, which was sad and sweet and touched him in a way he could not understand. He said nothing, and Ildera did not give any indication that the song affected him. The men continued most of the morning until they came into a small village, where they stopped for lunch. The people were friendly and kind, and some of them knew Ildera. After lunch, the travelers continued down some steps from the village on the remainder of an ancient-looking road. Then to Arden's surprise, they suddenly emerged on the edge of a cliff. The desert was so far below that getting down to it seemed impossible for them. The next surprise was a wooden house that was not a house but the housing for a great hoist and a large basket that could be lowered far below. The men at the house greeted Ildera, for they knew him, and agreed to lower the travelers down. Arden tried to hide his reaction, for he was afraid, having never seen anything like this way of traveling. Ildera and Arden entered the basket, and the men lowered them down. Arden held on and mostly looked at the floor of the basket. He could not tell how far he and Ildera went or how long the descent really took, but when they reached the bottom, they were much closer to the desert. He looked up and could barely see the house above, and he shivered.

Ildera seemed pleased, and he and Arden walked on a path down towards the desert. The trees gave way to tall grass, and the soil of the path became sandy. The sun was hot, and insects flew throughout the grass. The travelers continued downward, while the desert became closer with every step. The path met with a road, like the same ancient road above, made of grayish white stone. The road led back into some forest again before it went through a clearing and around what looked like a fountain. Water flowed out of it and ran off beneath the road off to the sides. Two great trees flanked the road ahead, and then steps ran down to the edge of the desert.

"We will stop here," said Ildera, making his way under the trees ahead. The men sat in the shade on some large stone ruins in the grass, and a warm breeze blew from the desert. "We will stay here until nightfall, when you will leave. In the mean time, I will give you some instructions and introduce you to your traveling companion when he gets here. Come, let's walk down the stairs a bit, and I will show you something."

The travelers walked down the stairs halfway so that they could see out into the desert up close. Where the stairs on which they stood ended, another set rose up about ten feet to meet the desert surface. From that point, a road made of the same stone ran straight ahead as far as the eye could see. In the noonday sun, the road reflected a shining, golden light.

"That road is the one you will travel," said Ildera, and he and Arden returned to the trees. "You must travel at night, and you can only take what you need. During the day, you can sleep in one of the many shelters along the road. You must carefully ration your food, and especially your water. In ten days, you will reach the only source of water in the desert. Normally, this crossing would not be possible for you, but you have the cakes from Jeveka, and Prisca has given you some fruit that you can eat that will help you greatly. Now is also early spring, not high summer when the desert gets unbearably hot. I cannot emphasize this warning enough, though: do not leave the road, no matter what." He continued dispensing advice as he took their packs, laid out everything that Arden would need for the journey, and went through each item in great detail. Arden did not even have the time to be nervous, and he really wasn't because of the confidence that Ildera had in him. As the travelers were finishing packing Arden's one small pack, they heard the cry of a bird approaching. Ildera stood and raised his arms. A large bird flew into the clearing and landed on the fountain. Ildera walked forward with joy and welcomed the bird. It flew from the fountain and landed on his arm. It was so large that Arden wondered how he could hold it up.

"Welcome, my friend," said Ildera, and the bird chirped in response. "Arden, this is the Ruach Bird, and he will join you and help you cross the desert." Arden did not know what to say. He was surprised and in a way disappointed, for he expected a man like Ildera to accompany him. Ildera laughed. "Hold out your arm," he said, and Arden did. The bird flew up in the air and when it landed on Arden's arm, it was only as big as a large robin. It just stood there, staring at Arden.

Arden finally said, "Hello."

The bird replied, "Greetings, Arden." Arden almost jumped when the bird spoke.

"You speak!" he said, startled.

"Of course I speak," said the bird.

Ildera laughed again. "Oh, I'm sorry, Arden, I should have told you, but meeting my friend is much more interesting this way. Come; let's sit down in the shade."

The bird flew from Arden's arm and perched next to the men on the grass. Now it was so large that it stood as tall as a man. Its feathers were brown with a mix of color in them, and its beak and eyes were black. The bird's majestic appearance would have scared Arden had he met it without warning.

"Well," the bird said, "the first question you're going to ask is why my size changes, aren't you?" Arden just nodded his head yes. "My size has to do with the measure of faith in each person on which I perch. Ildera has great faith, and yours is good for someone of your age. You also noticed, I'm sure, that in either case, you feel no burden from me. I can perch on the smallest child without causing harm. But I only go where I am wanted and needed." He paused but said no more, as if waiting.

"The Ruach Bird is the best companion one could have when traveling, especially across the desert," said Ildera. "He has helped me many times in the past, especially across the western mountains on the edge of the desert."

Suddenly Arden understood. "Will you cross the desert with me?" he asked; then he added, "I cannot cross alone, and I need your help."

"Of course I will come with you," said the Ruach Bird, and he sang a very short, sweet, joyous birdsong. Arden felt that the bird was smiling.

"What should we do now?" asked Arden.

"Rest," said the Ruach Bird. "I see a nice spot over here on the grass where you can lie down. Ildera, you should come as well. The sky is blue and pleasant. Sleep the afternoon in peace. I will sing for you."

"Thank you," said Ildera, almost reverently.

They lay on the grass, and for a moment Arden felt like he was home again in Caladen on the grass under the blue sky. The Ruach Bird sang a beautiful song, and Arden fell fast asleep. Ildera listened for some time as his mind wandered to many places. That kind of rest was better than sleep to him, but even he fell asleep eventually. The Ruach Bird grew in size until his wings were large enough to cover both men. Had anyone or anything malevolent lurked around, it stood no chance of harming the travelers while the Ruach Bird stood watch.

Eventually the sun sank lower in the sky as late afternoon became early evening. Both Arden and Ildera woke then and felt refreshed. They drank water from the fountain, and Arden filled his two large bottles of water. Each would fit on one edge of his pack. Ildera took food from his pack and shared a meal with Arden while the Ruach Bird stood nearby. When the meal was over, Arden knew that the time had come for him to leave. He was filled with great sorrow. He put on the sword, which had a strap on the sheath so that it would cross his back. His pack went on over the sword. The weapon made the pack a little uncomfortable, but as the pack was light, it was easily bearable. Ildera and Arden embraced and said farewell at the top of the steps.

"Thank you for everything," said Arden. "I shall never forget any of this journey."

Ildera said, "I am grateful that I have met you, Arden, and I am saddened at our parting. I do not know if we shall meet again, but I hope so. Remember why you are here, though, and the purpose of your journey: to meet the King of Kings. I have done the best I could to prepare you. Trust in the Lord Most High and His Spirit."

Arden put on his pack, and he and Ildera walked down the stairs together and then up the smaller set to the edge of the desert. The sun was beginning to set, but the road still shone straight ahead. The Ruach Bird flew above them on the wind, surveying the desert ahead.

"Farewell, Arden," said Ildera, and Arden started off. Ildera called from behind: "Listen to the Ruach Bird. And do not stray from the road. May the Lord Most High bless you and protect you on your journey!"

Arden continued walking on the stone road, which was flat and easy to follow even as the sun set and night came. The stars glittered brightly, and the road still shimmered in their light. The Ruach Bird had long since landed on Arden's shoulder. It did not say too much, but the knowledge that he was not alone was comforting to Arden.

Ildera walked back up the steps and watched for as long as he could see Arden and the bird. Then he stood for a while longer, until the sun had completely set. He would make his way back to Beriya in the morning; so he spent the night in the clearing. For several hours, he stared up at the stars, lost first in thought and then in prayer. The next day, he returned to Beriya and to the school. He purposed in his heart to leave as soon as possible to return to his home north of Jeshuryn by way of the western mountains. He enjoyed traveling but missed his home and even more the woman to whom he was betrothed. When he reached the dam, he looked out in the fields and saw Jeveka and Colley walking with a woman. Ildera narrowed his eyes against the sun to see the woman better. She was his betrothed! When they saw each other, they both ran across the field to embrace.

"But how?" he stammered in surprised. Jeveka and Colley both had gleeful grins on their faces, and they were looking behind him. He turned around and found his answer.

Chapter 18

Arden's Choice

The first part of the desert crossing was easy. The desert was surprisingly cool at night, and Arden found that following the road was easy. It was flat and ran straight for as far as the eye could see. Compared to the journey from the crossroads to Beriya, walking along this road was much easier. Many stone buildings stood along the road, and when the sun rose, he knew that he had to stop for the day. He was uncomfortably hot in the buildings where he took shelter, but he was still cooler than he would be facing the hot sun. Because nothing lived in the desert, no insects bothered him. The Ruach Bird told him that the desert was completely lifeless, as the Lord Most High had declared it would be. The only source of water, which was aptly named the fountain of life, only flowed because the Lord Most High declared that it would. The Ruach Bird instructed Arden to eat one of the cakes each morning before going to bed along with only one mouthful of water. Later, Arden could drink more water, but no more than a mouthful at a time. Just before the sun began to set, Arden and the bird would set out. During the night, he would eat one of the pieces of fruit that Prisca had given him. The fruit seemed to keep him from being thirsty. By now, the mountains behind him were out of sight, and the flat desert surrounded him. The third day, after he had fallen asleep, the Ruach Bird carried him a great distance to another shelter. Without that help, he would not have been able to last across the desert. By the morning of the ninth day, one water bottle was completely empty, and the other had no more than two mouthfuls left. The wise counsel of the Ruach Bird had helped Arden conserve the water. Many times Arden wanted more than just a mouthful of water, and he would have taken it if not for the presence of the Ruach Bird. He did not realize how far he had come and how far he would have had to go if he had no help. He was unaware that the Ruach Bird had carried him during the day for five days. The morning of the tenth day, Arden came upon the vast ruins of a city. The city was called Meresham, and the road before it passed by the stone columns of an ancient gate. Nearby, two roads split off to the sides at an angle.

"The fountain is straight ahead," said the Ruach Bird. "You're almost there."

Arden was happy, because he had drunk the last of the water several hours ago and he was starting to get thirsty. The road expanded to three times its former width, and it ran straight into a large square with the fountain at the center. Water flowed gently from the fountain, and Arden was able to drink and refresh himself. The bird directed Arden to stay nearby, and he was able to drink his fill and then fill the water bottles before he left. When Arden and the Ruach bird were out of the city, the road continued as before, and the same pattern of travel continued. Although Arden did not realize the change, every day he was making less progress as his fatigue was growing.

On the fourteenth day, no shelter was near except for a small wall. The flat landscape had changed to a desert with great sand dunes all around. Yet the road remained clear.

Arden was distressed at the lack of shelter, and anger rose from somewhere within him. Normally, the Ruach Bird would have just sheltered him with his wings, but Arden's lack of faith made such an arrangement impossible. The state of Arden's faith was so bad that Arden could not understand the bird; he only heard chirping and didn't realize that the Ruach Bird was trying to speak to him. He slept behind the wall as best he could, but his face and arms were sunburned. The damage would have been much worse had the Ruach Bird not awakened him. He sat up, startled, and felt the heat of the sun on his face. The Ruach Bird was as small as a sparrow, and Arden took a minute to realize what had happened. He felt the conviction and guilt in his heart and repented. When he said he was sorry, the Ruach Bird grew larger, and Arden could understand him again. The damage was done, though. His face and arms burned as he walked in the night. He felt stupid at yet another failure and said so.

"Life has some hard lessons to learn," said the Ruach Bird, "especially the ones that we learn the hard way when we didn't have to."

Arden felt better, and the next three days, he found shelter in small buildings by the roadside. Despite how tired he was, the sunburn kept him from getting comfortable, and his sleep was not as satisfying as it had been. On the seventeenth day, Arden and the bird reached another area of large, stone ruins. This time, Arden could see two small towers ahead on each side of the road. It was almost morning, and the sun would rise very soon. Arden decided to make for the towers, because he would most likely find a place to shelter there. The Ruach Bird had flown ahead, and Arden could see him flying over the towers. As Arden got closer, he passed many stone foundations and saw that the land dropped off ahead. The sun had just come up when he reached the towers. They had the same golden glow as the road in the morning sun. He saw that they were actually at the end of a bridge that spanned across over what once must have been a decent-sized river. He could see two other towers at the other end of the bridge. But the bridge itself did not look very safe. It was made of stone and wood, but from the near end Arden could see that the middle span had mostly collapsed or been worn away. The towers were mostly intact. The one on the right was in better shape, and it seemed like a good place to rest. The Ruach Bird came back and landed on the bridge near Arden.

"The towers on the other side are in better shape. Why don't you cross the bridge and rest there?"

"Can I get across the middle span? It doesn't look safe."

"A wooden beam remains on the left where you can walk safely. It is narrow, but the railing will hold you if you need support."

Arden started across the bridge. He did not like walking over the wooden beams, because they looked weak and creaked with each step. Slowly, he reached the middle. Then he noticed how far below the ground was. His heart pounded with fear, and he could not make himself go forward.

"I can't do it," he said. "Can I walk down below instead?"

"You can cross this bridge," said the Ruach Bird encouragingly as it landed on the railing. "Getting off the road would not be wise. Just grab the railing with your left hand, and walk across towards me. Don't look down; just concentrate on the other side."

Arden grabbed the end of the railing with his hand, but he could not make his body go forward. He was frozen with fear, and his breathing was heavy. He had to step back onto the creaking wood and then walk back to the towers the way he had come. He looked over the edge, and he could see that the former river bank was not too steep and that he could go down that way. He could hear Ildera's voice in his head telling him to listen to the Ruach Bird. He felt ashamed at his fear and lack of trust. The Ruach Bird flew back and landed on the railing nearby.

"It's all right, Arden," said the Ruach Bird. "Just wait for a few minutes, and then you can try again. But you need to cross soon before the sun gets much higher."

But Arden had already decided not to cross the bridge, and he walked around the tower to see what was under the bridge. A path led down to the base of the bridge. From there, he could walk underneath it, where he probably would be in the shade most of the way. He used that advantage to rationalize his decision.

"I'm sorry," he said. "I can't go across. I will walk down below the bridge."

"Arden, wait," said the Ruach Bird, but it was too late.

Arden felt guilt in the pit of his stomach for not listening to the Ruach Bird. Had it not guided him and carried him safely so far? He could not explain why he did not even want to talk about crossing the bridge, for the fear of it overcame his reason. He heard in the back of his mind the Queen telling him that he would die in the desert. He reached the bottom of the bridge easily and felt some renewed confidence. A clear path seemed to stretch under the bridge behind each foundation. He looked around, but the Ruach Bird was nowhere to be seen. As he walked out from under the first span to get a glimpse above, he sank to his knees in loose sand and fell over. He was startled but did not move. He managed to get up and walk back to the solid ground under the bridge. He felt foolish and a little scared, and he hoped that the Ruach Bird had not seen him. He continued forward with caution and reached the next foundation. Some debris lay ahead, which Arden could see was part of the middle span that had fallen from the bridge. But he could see that the crossing to the next foundation on the other side was significantly larger. He started across, only to find that the ground was less solid. He was ankle deep in loose sand. The ground got worse as he got closer to the center. Now the sand was almost up to his knees. But he reached the debris in the middle. He climbed up on a solid block of stone that had fallen. Another block lay ahead, and he slowly slid off the block where he was standing into the sand to walk to the next block. But the sand was deeper here, above his knees. He panicked and ran to the next block and climbed on it. When he stood on top of it, he saw several large, wooden beams that had fallen from above. The ones that he saw must be resting on others below, he thought. However, crossing them seemed even more perilous than crossing the bridge above. Part of him said to turn around and go back, but he still pressed on. He gingerly walked across the wooden beams to the next foundation. He tested the ground, which appeared to be solid. He slowly walked over to the last support foundation. He had taken some time to get this far, and the sun was already over the horizon. Arden stopped to rest for a second and compose himself. Looking ahead, the ground under the bridge seemed solid; it did not look like loose sand. However, the bank on this side leading back up was much steeper than the bank on the other side, almost a cliff. Worse, on both sides of the solid ground was loose sand. He could see now how the sand had blown around the bridge except for the patch ahead of him. He walked straight ahead on solid ground. But when he reached the bank, it was too steep to climb. He would have to walk out to the left or the right until he could find a place to climb. He chose the right side, and climbing was slow going. He was hugging the bank in front of him while the sand was getting deeper. He found some handholds and began to climb up. As he looked up, he saw the Ruach Bird circling above him; he could not tell how big it was. He climbed up the first part of the steep bank and came to level ground. He walked forward and saw that he needed to climb up another steep bank. As he started up, he lost his hold and fell backwards, landing on the ground. He was not hurt, but the fall frightened him. With renewed adrenalin, he quickly climbed out and rolled over the edge onto the flat ground. He was sweating and tired. The hot sun had now risen fully, and the sunlight burned him so badly that he made his way into one of the towers and slumped to the ground. As he took the pack off, he noticed it was wet. Then with panic he realized that the fall had broken his water bottles. All of the water save a tiny mouthful was gone. He sat on the ground in a daze. The stupidity of what he had done was worse than the incident three days ago. Did he have to learn another hard lesson the hard way? The realization of his error was like a slap to the face, and a deep sense of guilt and embarrassment filled him. He felt tears coming, and he gave himself up to them. He put his head in his hands and sobbed. Somewhere in the midst of his crying, he felt the presence of another. The Ruach Bird perched there in front of him. It was as tall as he was sitting, and it looked sad, if that was possible.

Arden didn't know what to say, but he said, "I'm sorry. I really am sorry." The bird said nothing but moved closer. Arden reached forward and hugged him. Tears still filled his eyes, but he felt a release and some peace from having spent his grief.

The Ruach Bird spoke softly and gently. "Sleep now, while the cool of the morning remains. We will take stock of the situation when you wake up."

Arden slept for most of the day, longer than he had in the past week. When he woke up, he went outside. The day was giving way to early evening, and the Ruach Bird was perched nearby. Arden approached and said, "I don't know what to say."

The Ruach Bird said, "I'm disappointed that you chose not to listen to me. I cannot make you do anything that you don't want to do, although I hoped that you would at least talk to me. However, I am not angry. I can see now that you were weary and that the seed that the queen planted in your heart has taken root. Yes, I was there in the trees above you when you took the test. The choice is still yours: trust in the Lord Most High and live, or believe lies and perish."

Arden said, "I want to live and trust in the Lord Most High."

"Good," said the Ruach Bird. "Now eat two of the cakes now and save the other for tomorrow. You have one fruit left, and that will be for the third day. You can see now that our actions have consequences. Unfortunately, I cannot carry you now and make the journey easier. You can make the Lachmeth in three days, but your journey will be difficult. You will need to walk farther than you have done each day, and we will leave now, rather than waiting until sunset."

Arden ate the cakes and tried not to think about water. The Ruach Bird landed on his shoulder, and its presence brought peace.

"Take the remaining cake and fruit and put them in your pocket. Leave the pack behind. Take the sword with you. You will not need it in the desert, but it will serve you when the time comes. Now let's get moving!"

Arden left with renewed strength, and he walked the farthest he had gone in a single march, even more than on the first day. The next two days were tough. Distant mountains appeared on the horizon, but they still seemed impossibly far away, even after the first day. He was thirsty, and his mouth was dry. After the second night, his lips were noticeably more dry and cracked, and they bled. The third night, he continued walking despite his body's reluctance. Again, the Ruach Bird spurred him on. It quoted Scripture and told Arden a little about the land of Jeshuryn to keep him motivated. The next morning, the twentieth day, brought the mountains much closer. Arden could see that he had almost reached them. He had to reach Jeshuryn today; so Arden kept walking even as the sun rose. By now, his body was dehydrated, and he felt dizzy. He could see the walls of the Lachmeth before him, but every step forward became harder. The Ruach Bird had left to get help or something like that; Arden was getting incoherent. Finally, he lost his balance and tripped, falling forward. He caught himself and then knelt on the road. Finally, he collapsed.

Chapter 19

The Fortress Wall

The custom of the land of Jeshuryn was that, at seventeen years of age, you had to serve two years in the army. No exceptions were made for anyone, and even princesses had to go. Those in compulsory service spent most of this time in training, for no war had raged in over a thousand years. No one resented the custom of army service, and for many the time helped them to determine what they wanted to do in life. Personal bonds formed between these young soldiers, and those bonds remained for life, despite any distance. Because Caleb was older than Ariana, he left first, and his absence was hard for Ariana to bear. However, Caleb decided to stay in the army, and he had just become a junior officer in Ariana's second year of service. He was put in charge of Ariana's unit, and both siblings were happy with the arrangement. Ariana didn't get any breaks, but she didn't need any. She remembered the first month of her training when her class was learning fighting skills. She was paired up with a young man in one exercise on sword fighting who did not take her seriously, much to his regret.

At the beginning of her second year, the company went to the fortress at the desert wall, or the Lachmeth, as it was called, where the company would stay for a month before it then broke out into units for specialized training. The training was a little scary even after a year, but Ariana reminded herself, still amazed, that her older sister had gone through this experience unscathed. This reassignment was also a sad time, for the unit was going to break up when the soldiers got their new assignments. At the end of the evening, Ariana's unit and others gathered on the highest wall overlooking the desert. The sky was filled with bright stars on this night, and nobody minded standing in the warm breeze. The custom of the unit was to end each night in a song and prayer time. Then, the soldiers were dismissed until morning. At the time of songs and prayers, Caleb and Ariana would be allowed to break rank and lead the worship together.

Ariana sang:

The Lord is my light and my salvation;
    Whom shall I fear?
The Lord is the stronghold of my life;
    Of whom shall I be afraid?
When evil men advance against me
    To devour and destroy me,
When my enemies and my foes attack me,
    They will stumble and fall.
Though enemy armies besiege me,
    My heart will not fear.
Though war break out against me,
    I am confident in the Lord.

One thing I ask of the Lord;
    This is what I seek:
That I may dwell in the house of the Lord
    All the days of my life,
To gaze upon His beauty
    And seek Him in His temple.

For in the day of trouble,
He will keep my safe in His dwelling.
He will hide me in the secret place of His tent
And set me high upon a rock.

Then my head will be exalted
Far above my enemies who surround me;
At His tabernacle will I sacrifice
With shouts of joy!
I will sing and make music to the Lord.

What would have become of me
Had I not believed that I would see
The goodness of the Lord
In the land of the living?
Wait for the Lord; hope for and expect Him.
Be strong and brave, and take heart!

The Lord is my light and my salvation;
Whom shall I fear?
The Lord is the stronghold of my life;
Of whom shall I be afraid? [12]

When Ariana finished singing, the unit gathered together in a circle and held hands. Caleb started the evening prayer by giving thanks to the Lord. Then others could join in and speak any prayers that they wanted. When the individual speaking was finished, Caleb ended the prayer. The soldiers were now free to go to bed. Some lingered on the wall, looking out at the stars high above the desert. Sometimes, the soldiers all stayed together after prayer, talking into the night. Ariana did not stay tonight. She became tired during the prayer and wanted to sleep. The other nice thing about the fortress was not sleeping in tents. The fortress had a large room that was subdivided into small rooms so that each soldier had a private room of his own. Ariana's small room had a mirror, where she looked at herself and smiled. Her hair was totally messed up from the wind, and she would need to brush it. For a second, she tilted the mirror downward, and the pendant she wore flashed brightly. She took it off and held it in her hand as she sometimes would. *It is beautiful and Cali was beautiful,* she thought. She still did not understand why she had to wear the pendant, but she had promised that she would. She put it back on and went to sleep.

Ariana was the first to reach the wall at sunrise. She had time for a brief morning walk before breakfast. Today the view of the morning sky was spectacular, with a mix of blue, pink, and orange. She imagined for a minute that the desert was actually an ocean of water and that she was looking out over the sea from an island. She often tried to visualize what an actual sea of water would look like. A sea would make even the mightiest rivers of the land look like small streams in comparison.

A light breeze blew from the desert. A few morning birds flew along the cliffs after night hunting, while others would come out in the day. A bird landed nearby on the ground. It was one of the larger birds, and Ariana did not recognize what kind it was. It chirped and walked around looking at the ground, yet always keeping track of where Ariana was. Then it flew up from the ground onto the wall next to her. She was surprised that it showed such fearlessness as to come so close. At the same time, she saw how beautiful it was. She wanted to reach out and touch it. It sang a sweet-sounding song that was clear and piercing in its tone. The song it sang reminded her of something, but she did not know what.

Out of nowhere, she remembered a humorous play where a fair maiden walks along the wall, hoping to attract the attention of a guard with whom she has fallen in love. He is completely clueless, and unfortunately, three of his comrades-in-arms court her. She agrees to marry them, one by one, if they will prove their love for her by going out into the desert and bringing back some treasure, knowing full well that they will die in their quest. The guard she loves realizes, after spending the night lamenting the third death of a friend, that the test is impossible. He concludes, incorrectly, that the maiden hates all men, and he vows revenge. The misunderstanding all sorts itself out in the end. A child sees a bird walking on the wall, while four people sit nearby eating the morning meal. The conversation goes like this:

A CHILD: "Lady bird, lady bird, walking on the wall: who do you look for, out in the desert?"

PRIEST: "The prophets say, 'A man will come out of the desert, her true love, with the king's hand over his heart, and the spirit will hover over him like a great bird. He will faint at the gates, but she will give him water, and he will live.' Is this what you look for?"

WISE OLD WOMAN: "Be careful, dear bird, for others have waited their whole lives when no one has come."

MERCHANT (already drinking wine): "I saw messengers from the king pass through the gates, heading south on the desert road on a winter morn. An envoy they were, riding great horses. Is this what you look for?"

WISE OLD WOMAN: "The messengers will not return this way. They will come back from the north."

GUARD: "I saw a man walk out into the desert. He went to test himself and search for treasure in the ruins of cities long gone."

WISE OLD WOMAN: "That man is a fool; no one who goes into the desert alone ever comes back."

Ariana said to the bird on the wall, "Who are you looking for?" The bird chirped and flew away. She watched it fly away, and it headed straight out towards the desert. She followed it for some time as it flew lower until she saw another black speck behind it. Her heart skipped a beat, and she stood at the edge of the wall looking intently at whatever it was. It did not look like an animal but a man walking far below. Was it one of the guards or someone from the fortress? *It couldn't be,* she thought. *It must be someone from the desert. In any case, I must deal with it.* She turned and ran for the stable to get her horse. No one else was stationed on the wall to tell. As she ran around the corner, she almost knocked over two elders, dressed in white robes, who were not from the fortress. Their presence startled her more than seeing the man in the desert, and she was speechless. She did not have time to bow, because she ran right into them. The elders were a man and a woman, and the man grabbed her arm to keep her from falling. Both he and the woman smiled.

"Easy, child," said the man.

The woman handed her a canteen full of water and said, "Take this with you. Remember the mercy of our Lord. Now go, quickly!"

Ariana said nothing but ran to the stables. Attendants of the elders were there, and they had saddled Ariana's horse. She mounted him and rode down the street towards the gate. "Open the gate!" she yelled in her authoritative princess voice. The startled guards recognized her and opened the gate.

"What is it, lady?" yelled one of them.

"A man is coming out of the desert!" she replied.

"Wait, we'll get more men," the guard replied, but she was gone. The guards sounded the alarm, and soon the whole fortress was buzzing. Caleb was already awake, and he reached the stables as the guards arrived. They quickly saddled up and rode after Ariana, who had a fair lead by now. Her backup still had long way ahead to get to the desert. The road had several switchbacks leading down to the desert level, where a road led to the main road that went out into the desert from which the intruder was coming. Caleb could see that Ariana was already at the bottom of the switchbacks. He looked out to the desert. He did not see anyone, yet still rode on. As he made the second turn back towards the main road, he saw something on the ground out on the road. The shape was too far away to see what it was.

Ariana rode with fury out on the open road. She was angry inside at the thought of some outsider coming to attack her land. Her anger blinded her to reason, and the subconscious hatred of outsiders she had harbored for years came to bear in her heart. But the initial adrenalin rush was fading, and reason returned to her mind, which was full of questions now. What if she found more than one man? Surely by now other soldiers were following her as well. She did hear the alarm being sounded. Why were the elders at the Lachmeth? Why would the woman give her water? She was only going out a little way into the desert. By now she was approaching the main road, and she turned onto it. She was momentarily captivated by how straight and level it was, stretching out to the horizon. The morning sun which was just coming up cast a golden glow on the road. She looked ahead and did not see the man. Then she saw something on the ground. It was him. She approached and stopped still some twenty feet away. Was this figure on the ground some trick? Were more men hidden near him? She could see no one else in the area and no place for anyone else to hide. She dismounted and walked towards the man on the ground. She could hear the shouts behind her as Caleb and the guards reached the first road. They would be here soon, and their nearness gave her more confidence.

"Hey!" she shouted "You! Get up!" He did not move. She drew her sword and walked forward. To her surprise, she discovered the figure was not a man but an older boy dressed in a robe, not fighting gear. He was lying on his back, and his arms were stretched out. His hands were empty. He looked like he had a sword across his back. Keeping her sword pointed at him, she came even closer to look at his face. His skin was fair, and he had some sunburn from the desert. His lips were dry and cracked. He did not move at all. She stood in silence for a moment, thinking. Maybe this person was not part of an enemy invasion, but his presence here didn't make sense either. She sheathed her sword. If he was faking, well, she had a knife close at hand. He still didn't move. Then the thought occurred to her that maybe he was dead, or close to it. As she looked at his cracked lips, she became thirsty. Then she remembered the water. She walked back to her horse, still watching him but also seeing that the other guards were now turning on the main road and would be here in minutes. She took the water and walked back to him. "Remember mercy," the woman had said. *Those were strange words,* she thought. She came back and knelt beside his head. Slightly scared, she put the back of her hand on his forehead, which was hot to the touch despite the cool morning. She could see that he was breathing slow, regular breaths. She uncapped the canteen and took a sip of water for herself. Putting her hand behind his head, she lifted it up. The other men arrived at this point, with Caleb leading the way. He dismounted and drew his sword while the guard formed a perimeter around them.

"Ariana, what's going on? Who is he?" he asked.

"I'm not sure," she said, "but I think that he is not well and needs water." As she lifted his head up, he stirred slightly.

She put the water to his lips and gave him some. He drank a little and opened his eyes.

"Thank you," he rasped before passing out again.

"The area is secure, sir," said a guard to Caleb. "No one else is around."

"Very well," he replied. "Have four men ride down the road for half a league just to be sure."

"Right away," said the guard, who went to instruct the men.

"Let's take him back to the gate," said Ariana.

"Do you think that's wise?" said Caleb.

"The elders will know what to do. I saw two of them as I came down from the wall. One of them gave me the water to bring out here."

"I did not know the elders were here," he said. "Do you think you can lift him up to me on my horse?"

"It would be better if you put him on my horse," said Ariana. "I will take him back."

"Very well, I know there's no point arguing with you about it," he said, sheathing his sword.

"Quite right, brother," she said, smiling. "Help me get him up."

Chapter 20

The Boy from the Desert

Ariana was still holding Arden's head up, and Caleb bent down to lift Arden. He turned him sideways first and took off the sword. It was very light, and Caleb put it on his horse. Then he grasped Arden under his arms. When he picked him up, Arden's robe opened a bit, and the pendant he wore slipped outside. The jewels flashed in the morning sun. Ariana saw the flash of jewels and told Caleb to stop and hold the boy still. She took the pendant in her hand and looked at the jewels. His pendant was exactly the same as hers. The only difference was that this one was mounted in a silver metal, while hers was gold.

"I don't believe it," she said.

"Can you hurry up, please?" said Caleb. "He may look scrawny, but he's quite heavy."

"All right," said Ariana, and she got her horse and mounted it. Another guard had returned from the surrounding area, and he and Caleb were able to lift Arden up and place him across the saddle in front of Ariana, who helped pull him over. She started back at a walk so that the boy wouldn't get too shaken. Her mind was reeling from seeing the pendant. Caleb rode next to her.

"What's the matter, Ar?" he asked, seeing a puzzled look on her face.

"The pendant he's wearing," she said, turning to look Caleb in the eye, "is exactly the same as mine: exactly."

"The one that Cali gave you?" he asked.

"Yes," she said softly.

"How can that be?" he asked. "Do you think this boy is from Caladen? He looks like he could be. He is definitely a stranger to these lands."

"What does his home have to do with anything?" she asked. "Maybe the pendant is a popular design there. I'm sure all Caladenians can see the same stars there."

"Then why would I have to hide it?"

"I don't know. Maybe the elders will know, assuming that he is let into the fortress. I did not see a messenger from the City of Light."

"They have a way of mysteriously showing up at the right time," she replied.

"True," he said.

Sure enough, a messenger had arrived and declared that this stranger would be allowed into the land. Quite a crowd had gathered at the gates when Ariana and Caleb approached. The two elders, as Ariana would find out later, were named Seth and Mavis. Although the term "elder" did not refer to age, they were both well on in years, as most of the elders were. They both had gray hair and wore white robes.

"We have prepared a room for the boy, as you asked," said the commander of the fortress to the elders. He was sitting on his horse in full battle gear.

"Then let's bring him to it quickly," said Elder Mavis.

The crowd parted and let the commander through, followed by Ariana and Caleb and then the elders. The commander led the group to a place with quarters for guests. Surely the elders would be staying there as well. When the elders arrived, they took Arden down, carried him into a room, and laid him on a bed. Ariana was allowed in as well, and Elder Seth told her to give him more water, but only small sips at a time. Ariana was somewhat embarrassed by this task, still unsure of what to make of this boy. The commander stood at the doorway and reprimanded Caleb for letting his sister ride out alone.

"Commander," said Elder Seth, "we bid her to go in haste. I apologize for the breach of protocol." The answer satisfied the commander, to the relief of Caleb.

"Now, if you'll excuse us, we must attend to the boy," said Elder Mavis, politely dismissing the commander, Caleb, and even Ariana.

"But... there's something you should know," stammered Ariana. "He is wearing a pendant that is exactly like mine."

"Be patient, child, we'll take it from here right now," said Elder Mavis, and she dipped a cloth in water and placed it over Arden's forehead.

Elder Seth gently took Ariana's arm and led her to the door. "Thank you for rescuing him," he said, and he smiled. The next thing she knew, she was outside, still in a daze. The guards who rode with the elders were now stationed outside these quarters. Ariana remained unfocused for the rest of the day.

Later on, before the evening meal, Caleb found Ariana by the wall again. He was surprised that she was not in a good mood.

"Just like that," she said, "I save the boys' life, and they just take him away. 'We'll take it from here,' they said."

"What does it matter?" asked Caleb.

"Don't you want to know who he is and what he is doing here?" she replied.

"Not really," said Caleb. "I'm more interested in getting the duty roster set for next week at the moment." Ariana grumbled at his response. "Ar, what is it with you? The boy is none of our business. If it's the pendant, then talk to one of the elders. Surely they will know."

"It's just that...." She broke off. "Never mind," she said, "you're right. It's been a strange day, that's for sure," she laughed. "I'll meet you down in the mess in a few minutes."

Caleb laughed briefly and walked away. He was not convinced that Ariana was telling the truth. The boy and his pendant still bothered her for some reason. He knew that in times like these, her heart was hidden from him, and his best course of action was not to ask questions that would drive her deeper into seclusion. *I guess I am like that, too, in some ways, but usually when it concerns Beth. Oh well, I'm sure she will tell me when she is ready,* he thought, and then he joined some others as they went to the evening meal.

Arden took a few days to recover and get back on his feet. Not much about him was known, and rumors spread about the visitor from the desert. The elders did confirm that he was from Caladen but said little more, except he was welcome in the land and that soldiers should not be spending their time gossiping. The elders attended him and prayed for him. They also welcomed him and promised to take him to the City of Light. They knew that they were supposed to do so, but not why. Arden confessed that he had been exiled and told them much of his travels. Others were around, and some of them heard parts of his story. The public disclosure did not satisfy Ariana's curiosity. She was able to find out that the boy was an exiled criminal, but she heard no detail except that he was to be taken to the City of Light. He certainly did not look like a criminal, and the contradiction made her more frustrated at a partial story.

Much to Ariana and Caleb's surprise, the elders summoned them to the office of the commander of the fortress. They were told that they were to be part of the escort that would take this young man, Arden, north to the city of Arkadelphia, outside the City of Light. The siblings would not just be representing the military, for as royal heirs, their duty was to go. Secretly, Ariana was happy, because she wanted to know more. Caleb was not happy, for this assignment would take him away not only from his command but also from Beth. Both brother and sister said nothing except for a simple acknowledgment of their orders. As they were leaving, the elders were walking out. Ariana had to ask her question.

"Excuse me, elders," she said, surprising Caleb.

"Yes, child," replied Elder Mavis.

"Can you please tell me why this stranger is wearing the same pendant that I have?"

Both elders looked at each other before responding. "That answer is for the future," said Elder Seth.

"I'm sorry," said Elder Mavis, "but that is all we can say."

"And part of the reason is that we do not know," said Elder Seth gently. "Many things happen, and though we only see a glimpse of them, we know that they must be. We trust in the Spirit of the Lord Most High, as you must as well."

"We would ask that you not speak of this coincidence to anyone, for words, although seemingly meaningless, can travel far and wide with great consequences," said Elder Mavis.

"When do we leave?" asked Caleb.

"Tomorrow morning," said Elder Seth. "We are waiting for another party to arrive and join us on this trip north. I think that you will be happy when you see them."

Later that afternoon, guards spotted a group of travelers approaching from the northeast. Riders went out to meet them, and the guards and travelers rode back together. Ariana and Caleb were on the wall they approached, but the travelers went straight to the elders. Missing the newcomers did not really matter to Ariana, for she was too busy thinking of many things and staring out at the desert. Caleb was farther down the wall with Beth. He would only be gone twenty-one days or so, but the separation would seem longer to him and Beth. Ariana was so lost in thought that she did not even hear the people approaching from behind her.

Suddenly a voice said, "I travelled all this way, and you would think that my niece would be the first to greet me."

She turned in surprise. "Uncle Hershel! What are you doing here?"

Hershel and his sons had come, and other soldiers were walking with them. "See how she greets me? Not even, 'Happy to see you Uncle,'" he laughed to the others with them. Ariana ran and embraced him. He kissed her on her forehead.

"It seems that we are going on a little trip north together," he said.

Chapter 21

The Road to Arkadelphia

The journey north was only ten days but to Arden the journey seemed so much longer. Hershel told Arden of his journey after their parting at the crossroads but it was mostly uneventful. As Ildera had said, a force had ridden after them and split at the crossroads. They easily overtook Hershel's wagon but after a quick look at the occupants kept going. When they came to the city of Kish west of Ashkelon, there were checkpoints on the roads with the Queen's soldiers. They claimed to be looking for a criminal and the irony made Hershel chuckle. Again, they paid no heed to Hershel, the old woman and her grandchildren. As if by good fortune, they stopped for the night at a small inn where several of the soldiers were staying. As Hershel had a way with people, he was able to talk with them. They were frustrated and not really interested in looking for some boy from Caladen but they dared not disobey the Queen. Hershel found out that they had sent troops and spies to every port as well, especially Nescor. They also gained support from the neighbors to the north to watch the road to Jeshuryn. Other than that the Queen could do very little. Hershel knew that she could never enter Jeshuryn and would not dare to send troops near there. But she would never give up and heads would roll when Arden was not found. He did not share that revelation with Arden. He also knew the Queen would never consider that he could have made it across the desert and as far as she knew the lands to the south west were deserted wilderness and only a fool would go there.

Ariana was curious as to why her Uncle Hershel was there.

"I made a promise to see that Arden arrives safely at the City of Light," was his reply.

As they continued on Arden was filled with nervous expectation which increased each day. At first he realized he had not felt this way since the day he met Sarah: the excitement and the expectation of seeing her again. He was happy that his destination was close at hand and that he would be able to return to her again. Or would he? The realization dawned on him that, in this entire journey, he never really thought about what he would say to the King of Kings. He assumed he would just apologize and would be able to go. But that outcome was not a sure thing.

On the third day, this reality sank in hard, and Arden's cheerfulness turned into depression. He looked around him at the people in the party riding north. Next to him rode the girl Ariana, or princess, he corrected himself, who looked like she would cut him down with her sword should he breathe wrong. Riding between Arden and the princess was her brother Caleb, who seemed like he did not really want to be present. He was not rude to Arden, but he said very little. Two of the elders' guards led the group with Hershel's sons. The guards were friendly to Arden, and the sons had sailed with him from Caladen. Their kindness made Arden feel better, but Hershel and the two elders, who rode behind him, were the only ones he really trusted. Behind the elders and Hershel were the other two personal guards. Arden could see the elders' guards talking with Hershel's sons up ahead, and though occasionally he would hear Hershel laugh behind him, he could not hear the conversation. Ariana and Caleb said very little except to each other, and the ride was relatively quiet. At first, this silence was fine with Arden, but on the third day, he was working himself up with despair and would have gladly welcomed any conversation. He was so distracted that he fell off his horse as the group was riding through large clumps of high grass. The horse was stepping around one of the clumps, but Arden was not paying attention and fell off. His fall startled Caleb's horse, which ran ahead as Ariana's did, too. Ariana drew her sword at the commotion and rounded on Arden. Hershel, who was in back talking to the elders, laughed out loud at first, but he bristled when he saw Ariana turn, and he rode to intercept her. Arden was unhurt except for his pride as he landed in the soft grass. He rose to find Ariana riding towards him, sword drawn.

But Hershel arrived first and rebuked her. "Niece, is this kind of reaction what you are learning in the army, to help a man who has fallen off his horse with a sword? I have sworn an oath to protect this young man, and the elders have welcomed him to our land. Why do you shame us with this behavior?" Ariana had a shocked look on her face at his words; then she angrily sheathed her sword and galloped forward to where Caleb was. Hershel helped Arden up, saying, "What troubles you, Arden, which would cause you to be so distracted?"

Arden explained his thoughts to Hershel. Only Hershel and the elders were close enough to hear him. Ariana and Caleb had ridden ahead next to Hershel's sons, and the guards were behind them. Hershel laughed gently, not meanly, at Arden's concerns.

"What do you think Ildera would do right now?" he asked.

"Be patient, I suppose, and trust in the Lord Most High."

"Excellent!" said Elder Mavis. "You have had a wise teacher."

"But patience in youth can be difficult," said Elder Seth, "and we have seven more days to go. Arden, you know that the King of Kings is just and fair, and His heart is merciful. Let that mercy be a comfort to you in the days ahead. Worrying about tomorrow or what might or might not happen is pointless. You knew that this day would come when you left your home, but you did not know how you would get here. From what I hear, the Lord Most High has certainly blessed your path with wise men and women that know His will. That care alone should give you great comfort and peace in your heart. I cannot tell you what will happen when you reach the City of Light or where your journey will lead, but you must have faith."

Arden felt reassured at these words, and the four riders had a lengthy discussion that dissolved the fear that Arden felt. For the rest of the day, Arden rode next to the elders and Hershel. When the group stopped for the evening, the elders prayed for Arden and laid their hands on him while the others set up the camp and made the evening meal. Then the elders went to each person and prayed for him, even their own guards. When the elders touched Arden, he felt peace wash over him from head to toe. He felt calm and joy back in his heart again. He truly repented in his heart for what he had done and thanked the Lord Most High for watching over him on this journey. Arden realized that he was truly blessed and that he never would have come so far without these wonderful people. When the time finally came for the evening meal, the travelers did not all sit together but sat scattered around the camp. Later, they would all sit by the fire before going to bed. Ariana cooked the meal tonight and brought food to everyone except Arden. Arden felt a momentary tightness in his stomach as Ariana took what looked like the last large plate of food for herself. But the plate wasn't for her alone.

She sat in front of Arden and put the plate between them. She took the surprised Arden's hands and said, "I apologize for my behavior and ask your forgiveness."

She paused and waited for Arden's response. Too shocked to speak for a moment, Arden finally said, "Of course I forgive you."

"Good," she said, "now let's share a meal together and make peace between us."

Arden and Ariana did not notice the others smiling when they heard this exchange. Despite her peace offering, Ariana still seemed cool to Arden. He was puzzled by her demeanor, for he had done her no harm. In fact, he evidently owed her his life, and this fact added more confusion to him. He found that he had nothing to say to her despite trying to think of something. This meal brought them face to face, which was the closest that they had been together, and they were both studying each other while trying not to make the examination obvious. Arden could not help noticing how pretty Ariana was. He suddenly thought that, if he were to mention her appearance, she would probably draw her sword again. He laughed to himself. That they would be friends in the short time remaining seemed improbable, but Arden guessed that Ariana would be a good friend. Ariana was more puzzled by Arden than he was by her. Arden seemed so open, honest, and friendly, qualities which did not fit her perception of an outsider, especially a criminal. Yet he was allowed in the land. He also did not look like someone who could cross the desert alone. Nothing about him made sense. And he wore the pendant. What could that pendant possibly mean? The elders said not to speak of the coincidence, but it was so strange. Then the thought came to her mind that only a few days were left in the journey, and then this stranger who shared her secret would be gone. What would be the harm if she asked questions? The elders did not tell her not to ask Arden anything.

"So, what did you do?" she asked.

"What do you mean?" replied Arden.

"I mean, why are you here? What did you do that you have to see the King of Kings?"

Arden felt his face turning red. "I sat on His throne," he said softly.

"What?" asked Ariana.

"A throne stands in the great Cathedral in Harran upon which no one may sit but the King of Kings. I sat on it, and now I must go and apologize and seek His judgement."

Ariana almost laughed out loud but did not because of the sadness in Arden's voice. Hardened criminal indeed! But she could see the sadness in him. "I'm sure that everything will be just fine," she said. The pair continued to eat in silence, but when they finished eating, they did talk a bit. Ariana asked Arden about the sea, for she had always wanted to see it. She still could not imagine an ocean of water with no land in sight. Hershel came over and joined in the conversation, and soon all three were laughing about things. Hershel had a way of turning any conversation into a positive exchange. Even Caleb came over and listened while Hershel told of his trip from Kadesh through Kiriatha down to the Lachmeth. His journey had been uneventful, but interesting. Soon the conversation group was called to clean up and prepare for the night. As everyone sat around the fire before retiring to sleep, Arden felt better and at peace.

That night, Ariana had a dream exactly like the vision she had seen during the festival as a child. She had completely forgotten about that vision until now. The vision started with a large crowd of people around her, yelling and cheering. She was standing on the edge of a cliff, and a battle of some kind was going on below which she could not see because of the crowd. A woman and a man stood next to her. She felt she knew them. Once again, fear started to rise within her. The woman put her arm around her. She felt that the woman was Cali and wanted to say something but couldn't. A young man stood next to her, and she grabbed his hand for comfort. Was the man Caleb? She could not tell. The stars on her pendant were shining brightly, and light shone from her and other two next to her. The light was so bright that she could no longer see the crowd. She woke to sunlight shining in her eyes.

The remaining days on the road passed quickly for Arden. He told the elders and Hershel of his journey, and Ariana and Caleb also rode with the group, listening intently. The elders were surprised to hear of the keepers and how Arden spoke of them so casually. They knew the legend, but nobody had ever seen them. For Ariana, hearing Arden's adventures was like listening to a tale of old, like a bedtime story. She unintentionally laughed out loud as Arden spoke of the Ruach Bird. Everyone turned toward her.

"Sorry," she said. "I just can't believe it. A talking bird helped you across the desert! What did it look like?"

Hershel gave his niece a disapproving look, but Arden continued. When he described the Ruach Bird, Ariana realized that it was the same bird that she saw on the wall. Her face turned red, and she did admit her realization to the group. Later, Caleb gave Arden his sword back. The two were able to practice a bit, and Caleb found Arden to be more skilled than he looked. Ariana was friendlier towards Arden as well, and the three of them rode together on the day the group reached a small town on a hill. To the right was a road leading northeast to the City of Light and the road they were on continued straight on to Arkadelphia. They stopped to rest there and have the noonday meal. Afterwards there was some discussion between the Elders and Hershel. The original thought had been to proceed to Arkadelphia and then go to the gates. Without warning another group of travelers rode into the village. Amongst them was none other than the King of Arkadelphia himself.

Elder Seth was talking to the king as Arden approached. Hershel was pointing out the road that led to the City of Light to Caleb and Ariana. Elder Seth motioned for Arden to join him.

"So, Arden, what do you think of this land?" Elder Seth asked.

Arden answered, "It's beautiful," and he was not lying.

"How long is the journey to reach the gates of the City of Light?" asked Hershel.

"If we all travel in a procession there," laughed Elder Seth, "the journey could take some time. However, I think that three younger people might ride there in an hour's time." As the elder said so, he put his arms on both Caleb's and Ariana's shoulders.

Ariana and Caleb were surprised and delighted and looked to their uncle for approval. "With the king's permission," he said, turning to the king.

"You have my leave," said the king, and he turned to Arden. "You need to go the southern lower gates. I think that you and your companions can find the way."

The other two went to fetch the horses, but Arden stopped. "Then, is this goodbye?" he said, not knowing what would happen.

"I don't know," said Hershel. Elder Seth was silent.

The king said, "You must go to the gates and see."

Chapter 22

The White Gates

Ariana and Caleb were on their horses, and they beckoned Arden to join them.

"Go on, my son," said Elder Seth with a smile. "And try to keep up with these two."

Arden ran to his horse, and all three young people left with a gallop. Elder Mavis came and joined the king and Elder Seth as they watched the three riders go down the road and across the fields.

Caleb raced down the road with Ariana behind him. Arden thought of Colley and the fun he had riding Ildera's horse. Arden was not too far behind, and eventually the siblings stopped and let him catch up. The trio continued at a walk through a small village. Straight ahead were the mountains that rose up sharply, and Arden could not ignore them. The road turned to the right, and he could see in the distance where it led up to the base of the mountain. The thought occurred to him that, even if he passed through the lower gates, he still had to travel quite a distance to the top of the mountain where the City of Light was. He was not sure if Caleb and Ariana would be allowed to go. He assumed that they would not be. Both Ariana and Caleb were talking and laughing and enjoying themselves. As the three got closer,

Arden felt a nervous excitement inside as well as a host of other emotions that overwhelmed him. He was finally here, and the moment of truth would come soon. Those thoughts were like a splash of cold water on his face. After a few minutes, Ariana noticed how serious Arden looked. She quieted down, and Caleb caught on and did the same. Caleb realized that, for him and Ariana, this trip was just another fun ride, but to Arden it was much more. Ariana wondered what would happen at the gate. The thought occurred to her that Arden would enter the gates, but she and her brother could not. Should they wait or go back to the city? She did not know and did not want to mention the possibility of leaving either. The three rode in silence for a while until they reached the turnoff that led to the gates, which was easy to find as they could now see the gates in the distance. Two guard towers stood on either side of the gates. The riders stopped for a moment to gaze at the view. Ariana took some water out and gave it to Arden to drink. Arden took a deep breath, exhaled, and drank.

"I'm sure that everything will be all right," she said. Caleb nodded in agreement.

"I guess we had better go then," said Arden.

The last stretch of road took only ten minutes. Arden was surprised at how big the gates were. Even Ariana and Caleb were impressed, for neither of them had ever been this close to the City of Light. The stone of the towers was like white marble, and the gates looked like they were made of bronze. A trumpet sounded while the riders were still five minutes away, and then three men came out from the guard tower to meet them. The men were wearing the same type of uniform as the messengers wore, but they wore bronze helmets and white uniforms instead of red ones to match the colors of the gate in their appearance. The guard in the middle had insignias on his uniform and helmet which led Arden to believe that he was the leader. The guards approached, and Caleb dismounted his horse. Ariana and Arden did the same.

"Hail, Arden of Caladen, Prince Caleb, and the Princess Ariana!" said the man in the middle. "We welcome you in the name of the King of Kings! I am Belden, the captain of the guard of the southern gates to the City of Light. We have been expecting you for some time. Come, this way," he said, motioning for the three to follow.

They said nothing, because they were very surprised.

"How was your journey?" Belden asked.

"Fine," they replied, still in amazement.

To the right of the gate in the corner of the tower wall was a small, square patio with a table and six chairs. The riders sat in the chairs, and the guards brought out water to drink and a tray with fruit and nuts to eat. Arden was not really hungry, but he ate some grapes out of politeness. The water was refreshing, for they sat in the hot sun. Usually a constant breeze provided relief, but at present the air was calm. The guards made small talk and inquired of the roads the riders took along the way. The conversation clearly implied that the guards knew all about the journey. The guards were polite and joyous in their manner, and most of the fear that Arden initially felt melted away.

Finally, Belden said, "Arden, tell us why you are here."

Arden cleared his throat and said, "I have come to see the King of Kings to ask His forgiveness and await His judgment." He tried to say these words with an official-sounding voice, but his voice seemed small in the presence of the gates and towers.

"Well said," said one of the guards. The others nodded in agreement.

"I'm sure that by now you can imagine that we already know of your quest," said Belden. "We have been anticipating your arrival for some time. Had you journeyed straight from Tyre, you would have been here a month earlier, and things would have been different. However, you seem to have taken the right path." He looked at Caleb and Ariana as he said the last part, but mostly at Ariana. Both of Arden's companions remained silent.

"Will I be allowed to enter the city and see the King of Kings?" Arden asked.

"I'm afraid not," said Belden. At this news, Arden's heart sank in despair. Ariana and Caleb were both surprised as well. Belden raised his hand before they could say anything. "You see, Arden, the King of Kings is not here. He has just left for Caladen, for now is the appointed hour for Him to go there. However, he bids you to join Him there, and He has sent a message to the king of Arkadelphia, who will help you start your voyage home."

Chapter 23

Cali's Fate

After a night of fitful sleep, Cali awoke to a cool morning breeze. A week had passed since the festival, and she felt weary. The vision that had kept her going was now fulfilled, and she felt like the wind had gone out of her sails, throwing her into depression. She was hungry, yet when she thought of food, her appetite left her. Last night Miriam had made a wonderful-smelling soup that reminded her of the soup that her mother had made when she was a child. She thought she could eat it, but when one taste brought back memories of home that made her sick at heart, she could not eat. Now she was folding her clothes, and the task reminded her of the day she packed to leave Caladen. She could almost hear her mother crying in the other room. How Cali had hated her. *Hated!* The memory was almost too much to bear now, but her mind continued in it. She had hated them all: the self-righteous and pious people who had judged her and the other five. Only now she knew that this view of them wasn't true. They loved her and wanted her to stay. But all Cali had wanted was to get out of there and to be with Rya, her beloved.

That her sole desire now was to see her mother again for one last time seemed ironic to her. She knew that her wish was impossible, and she had already made her decision anyway. Today was the day when she would normally go looking for stones; so going to the bridge would not seem out of place. She felt a lump of guilt in her throat as she left the note on her desk. Miriam and Hershel were both gone from the house now. If they had been home, she probably would not have been able to leave. Tears welled in her eyes, but she wiped them off and took a deep breath. She stifled any remaining tears and walked out of the house.

As she walked slowly to the bridge, everything around her seemed to be in a blur. When she reached the bridge, she walked out towards the center of it. The guards on duty waved, but they were in the middle of some conversation and took little notice of her. At the middle of the bridge was a span made from wood rather than stone like the rest of it. Again she encountered another guard house, but the gate was open because two of the guards, including the one that liked her, had walked across to the other side. She passed through the gate unhindered, as normal. Here the river was deeper and swifter, and the bridge was higher. As she walked up the span, her heart was pounding, and she fought back tears. At the very top, she tried to look back towards the village that had been her home for a brief time but could not see it. She turned and walked to the other side of the bridge. Gently but firmly, she grabbed the wooden railing and support beam and climbed up on the railing. She looked down at the rushing water far beneath her feet, and the height made her dizzy. Then she stared out across the river, and tears flowed down her face.

She said out loud, "Father in heaven, King of Kings, I have sinned against You and against my family and friends. I am truly sorry for what I have done, from the bottom of my heart. Ariana has told me of Your love and mercy. Please forgive me. Spare me from the punishment that I deserve. Please somehow let my mother know that I love her."

Then she closed her eyes and let go. She could not help but open them as she fell towards the water. Time seemed to slow, and a strong wind blew over the water that somehow slowed her descent. The strong wind also made the guards turn and look just as she jumped from the bridge. Her mind was blank, and she felt a peace about her in knowing that her life would soon be over. Finally, she hit the water and plunged beneath the surface. She was shocked at how cold the water was, even in the midst of summer. That thought was the last she had before losing consciousness.

She awoke and found herself breathing face down on the ground. Her body was burning with heat like a fire. For one second, she wondered if she was at the gates of hell. She raised her head and found that she was lying in the circle she had found as a girl that had been in so many visions and dreams. Instead of the small flower, she was in the center. The thorns that had been close to the center were burned to the ground, their charred ruins visible. Behind them were large, dark trees, and a gray sky was overhead. She felt more than saw a presence near her and realized that she was not alone. A man dressed in white stood inside the circle. The light seemed to radiate from Him. She could hardly look at His face, because so much love was radiating from it, and she could not speak. He came over to her and, taking her hand, helped her to her feet and embraced her. She felt tears pouring down her face, tears of sorrow and a joy that she could not explain. Finally, the man in white released her from the embrace, although the only reason she could stand was because He was still holding her.

She managed to say timidly, "Who are you?"

"I am the King of Kings," He said with a gentle voice.

She sank to her knees and felt so ashamed. She tried to say how sorry she was, but the words did not come out, just a pitiful gasp as she sobbed.

"Yes, I am the King of Kings," He said again. "And I have been given all authority by My Father in Heaven. All who call upon the name of the Lord Most High shall be saved. You have called upon Me, and I am here. Look at Me, child."

She lifted her eyes and gazed upon a face full of compassion and mercy.

"Your sins are forgiven, My child," He said as He pulled her up to her feet. "He who the Son sets free is free indeed." Suddenly, He gave shout like thunder: "Be cleansed from unrighteousness!" Immediately, the dark trees vanished and were replaced with grass. The charred thorns became flowers. The sky was blue, and the sun was shining. Now that the trees were gone, she could see that they had blocked out surrounding meadows that were full of flowers with butterflies around them and birds singing. The sight was joyous and glorious. She was suddenly aware that this was a King of power and authority, not the weak man she had thought at one time. That thought vanished as her past was washed away. It became like a story that you could tell about someone else, disconnected from the present.

"What is this place?" she asked without thinking.

"This is you," He said. "This is your heart."

"What happens now?" she asked. "I am dead? Is this heaven?"

"No, My child, it is not heaven, and you are not dead. You still have a part to play. Be comforted though, for I am with you and will never leave you. I have always been here, waiting for you, and now at last we are together." And with that declaration, the light began to fade along with the vision. Cali felt joy and peace like she never had before. Darkness surrounded her. Then slowly the darkness receded, and light appeared. She could hear the sound of water. She slowly became aware that she was lying on the ground and that the light was the sun. She opened her eyes and found herself on the bank of a river. She took a moment to wake up and get oriented to her surroundings. She realized that she must be somewhere downstream on the great river north of Jeshuryn, but she did not know where. She stood up and realized that she was naked. She was not cold in the hot sun, but she immediately grabbed her shoulder out of instinct to feel the scars that she had always tried to hide. She gasped! They were gone. She felt her back, and the scars from the whips were also gone. She stood there looking at her arms and legs for signs of damage, but her body was completely healed. She went back to the water's edge to look at her reflection in the water. She was amazed at how she looked. Her youth was restored, and she felt clean and healthy. She was so joyous that she almost didn't hear the horses approaching.

She turned around, and she could see two horses riding across the fields towards her. One of the horses was brown and the other white, both stately looking. A man was riding on the white horse. She felt no fear as he approached. Yes, he was heading right towards her. The man slowed the horses when he came close, and then he stopped at the top of the river bank. He dismounted, went to the other horse, and removed a bundle from the saddle. He approached Cali and, bowing, placed the bundle before her. It looked like clothing, and she suddenly remembered that she was indeed naked. The man did not look at her body once but turned away and said, "Please dress, lady. I will wait for you by the horses."

Cali unraveled the bundle and dressed in clothing that was made from fine white material embroidered with gold which fit her perfectly. The man had moved the horses to a shady spot under the trees. He sat under the trees with a book in his hand. Worn with age and use, it was written in a language so old that few living could understand it. As she came near, she could hear him speaking in an odd language. When she was close, he stood up and bowed again.

"My name is Ildera," he said. "I greet you in the name of the King of Kings, who sent me here to find you. It would be an honor if you would accompany me."

"I'm Cali," she said, and she didn't know what else to say except, "Thank you." So she smiled.

"You're welcome," he said, smiling back at her.

Taking her by the hand, he helped her up onto the horse. "Come," he said, "we have much work to do." They rode away across the fields together.

The End

Endnotes

1. Proverbs 8
2. Proverbs 14:5-11
3. Proverbs 14:12-15; 16:1-3
4. Proverbs 16:4-9
5. Proverbs 1:20-33
6. Proverbs 16:10-17
7. Proverbs 9:13-18
8. Proverbs 1:8-19
9. Psalm 1:1
10. Psalm 1:3
11. Proverbs 4:23 paraphrased
12. Psalm 27 NIV and AMP

9 781615 794423